Macabre Collection
Volume One

A.S.Chambers

This edition published in 2022.
Copyright © 2022 Basilisk Books.

*Teeth, Extraction, 53, Bell Court, Dog Days, Biscuit Tin of Doom, Scratchcard
Man* all previously published in *Oh Taste And See* © 2014.
*Relic, Test Flight, Second Time Around, Needs Must, Just Like Everybody
Else, Prodigy* all previously published in *All Things Dark And Dangerous*
© 2015.
*Matilda, Humble Pie, Smoking Is Bad For Your Health, Armitage, My
Divergent Lands* all previously published in *Let All Mortal Flesh* © 2016.

Cover art © 2022 Jens Rother

ISBN: 978-1-8384573-5-8

Dedication

For everyone who has given me support, help, advice and
numerous cups of coffee over the past ten years.
You have my eternal gratitude.

Also, special thanks to the Seraph tier members of my
Book Club for their valued support:
Paul Lewis
Gemma Innes.

For more details about my Book Club and how you can
receive signed copies of my books when they are
published, please visit my website:
www.aschambers.co.uk.

Ebook short stories.
High Moon - 2013
Girls Just Wanna Have Fun – 2013
Needs Must - 2019

Novellas.
Songbird – 2019
Bobby Normal and The Eternal Talisman - 2021
Bobby Normal and the Virtuous Man - 2021
Bobby Normal and the Children of Cain - Due 2022

Omnibuses.
Children of Cain - 2019

CONTENTS

Teeth

"Blasted chompers!"

McMillan yanked the offending dentures out of his mouth and hurled them with disgust into the porcelain washbasin, bloody spittle trailing behind them. He wiped the loathsome drool from his chin with the callused heel of his hand and peered into the brightly lit mirror. Using his gnarled, arthritic fingers he prised his lips open to survey the painful damage. Impatiently tugging the fleshy material this way and that he sneered at the red, weeping sores that peppered his inflamed gums and huffed in disgust, causing a glob of red muck to splatter against the otherwise pristine mirror.

He turned and opened the medicine cabinet, rummaging through his wide selection of pills and potions until he came upon the bottle of antiseptic. He diluted it down in a tumbler and swilled the vile-tasting concoction around his lacerated mouth. The release of the liquid into the basin coated the ill-fitting dentures in a wicked-looking red foam that gave the false teeth an air of malicious intent.

McMillan stared down at the teeth.

The teeth stared up at McMillan.

The old man's will broke first. He scooped the dentures up and sluiced them out under the cold tap before dunking them in an already prepared bowl of Steradent for the night.

"Your days are numbered, you evil little bastards," he promised stomping out of the bathroom and flicking off the light.

From inside the bowl, the teeth just grinned.

McMillan lay back, his twisted fingers clenching the black plastic and the bright light burning down into his eyes. He breathed shallowly through his nose as the dentist poked and prodded, ummed and ahhed, muttered and tutted. The green mask that pulsed back and forth over the dentist's mouth with his breathing combined with the large lens over his eyes made him look rather like some curious insectile creature exploring for a warm cavity wherein it might lay its eggs.

Or perhaps that was just McMillan's deep-rooted fear of dentistry that had led him to lose his original teeth in the first place.

He closed his eyes, continued to breathe shallowly through his nose and imagined himself to be elsewhere; a nice warm beach, an iced cocktail and the sea susshing on the shore. Yes, that was where he was, not in the black chair of a London specialist being sized up for thousands of pounds worth of treatment.

Eventually, McMillan felt the dentist pull away and the seat started to rise back to the seated position. He opened his eyes and clearing his throat asked, "Well? What do you think?"

The dentist removed his mask, revealing his

short, greying goatee which he stroked thoughtfully as he seemed to weigh up the options. "All in all I think we can create a new set of teeth for you, Mister McMillan. Your bones are quite worn down, but that is usual for your age and lack of teeth. However, dental science has advanced incredibly in the last few years and we can quite literally perform wonders."

"Yes, yes, yes," McMillan grumbled, "wonders, I'm sure. But will I have a full set of teeth again? My own teeth?"

"Sir, when I am finished, you will be the proud owner of the finest teeth that you will ever have laid eyes on."

Crunch!

A wonderful noise.

Crunch!

An explosion of pure taste unobstructed by a plastic plate.

Crunch!

McMillan sat back in the high-backed oak dining chair and regarded the slender stick of celery. How long had it been? How many years? He could not remember. He had been in his twenties when he had lost his first two teeth. It had been a bar fight, a brawl between two young bucks over some young beauty. That event had cost him physically, but the reward had been worth it. He had worn the gap as a medal of honour, displaying just how far he would go to get what he wanted, not just in the bar but also, later, in the boardroom. Some arrogant tosser would square up to him with an inane proposal as to where this business or that business should go and all he would do was smile at them. The gap between his top teeth was all that he needed to make them back down.

Other teeth had followed. He had been a busy man, that was what he had told himself over and over again. In his rational mind he had no desire to inflict the dentist's chair on himself unless it was absolutely essential. It was time-consuming and time was money.

That was what he had told himself. However, at the back of his mind, shrouded in a childhood fear, a set of painted, wooden teeth leered at him every time he felt a niggle in his jaw, every time a bowl of ice cream made him jolt in agony.

So it was that dread coloured his view of the world of dentistry and the trips became even less frequent, visiting only when the inevitable was required and teeth had to be extracted.

He finally relented to having bridges fitted in order to eat the foods that he liked, but he never found them to be satisfactory; the dental work would rock or rub against his gums. More often than not he would just do without when in private. As time went by his own teeth became fewer and the bridges became larger. His bottom set of teeth was the first to go and be replaced by a full denture. The upper set followed soon after. That had been about twenty years ago.

Twenty years of dull, boring slop and blistering, bleeding sores.

Not any more though. Not now.

McMillan polished off the crisp celery and turned to the bowl of radishes. He grinned with his new pristine teeth as he dropped one into his mouth and bit it viciously in half, a predator renewed with vigour and able to hunt once more. The sharp tang of the root vegetable made him moan with pleasure. This was the life. If only he had done this years ago, but the technology had not been around and he had been forced to endure the agony of the old plastic dentures.

When he had been younger, McMillan had always had a reputation for finishing off his meals first. He had been eager to get back to work, eager to get back and make money. Now, though, he sat and savoured every last mouthful. He rolled the masticated fibres around his liberated taste buds and savoured every last delicacy of their sweet, sweet flavours.

It took him almost an hour to consume a small salad. He would have been happy to make it last twice that long, but there was something else that he was desperate to reacquaint himself with.

Toffee.

McMillan looked at the small golden delicacy. He pulled on the fantails and the wrapper unfurled presenting the hidden treasure. With the utmost reverence, he lifted it to his nose and sniffed. Delicious aromas pirouetted in his nostrils, tantalising his senses and he felt saliva start to build up in his mouth. Carefully he peeled the sweet out of the wrapper and lightly held it between a gnarled thumb and finger before lowering it lovingly onto an accepting tongue.

He was sure that anyone passing his house would have been able to hear his moans of pleasure but he did not really care.

Flossing was a new experience for McMillan. He had never really seen the need for it before; a perfunctory scrub with a blob of minty toothpaste had been his oral routine once a day. Now, however, he had a considerable amount of money invested in his mouth and, like a stocks and shares portfolio, it needed care and attention.

At first he struggled with the white filament, his arthritis causing problems in gripping the long thread, but he persevered and shortly he was able to suck fresh air between his new set of perfect teeth. He grinned at himself in the bathroom mirror and ran his tongue over their surfaces. They felt so smooth, so clean. He could not remember a time when his mouth had looked like it belonged to a male model in a knitting pattern. All he needed was an Aran sweater and the obligatory hazel walking stick.

McMillan ran his hand through the thinning remnants of his grey hair and his eye caught a glimpse of pink and cream on the side of the washbasin. He picked the old dentures up and regarded them for a moment before a twinkle touched his eye and he grasped them between his curled fingers.

"Why, Howie," he voiced through the false teeth in a warbling falsetto, "how dashing you look."

"Why, thank you. I do believe I feel quite a spring in my step."

"Could it be that your life has suddenly improved for the better?" warbled the teeth.

"Indeed it has. Indeed it has. And do you know why?"

"Why no, we don't."

McMillan casually dropped the old dentures into the bathroom bin. "Because I don't need you pieces of crap anymore."

McMillan knew a lot of people his age had godawful trouble getting off to sleep. They'd lie there, tossing and turning, fretting about all sorts of daft rubbish. Did I leave the lights on downstairs? Did I lock the door? Will I wake up dead in the morning? He had no time for this whatsoever. Bedtime was sleep time and that was exactly what he did as soon as his head hit the pillow no matter what time in the evening it was. Having been the busy executive he had always cherished sleep. The more he got, the more fresh and alert he was for the killer deal the next day.

This evening was no exception, especially with the added bonus of a mouth that did not feel like someone had been stubbing out red hot cigar butts on his gums.

What was different this night was the dreaming.

McMillan never normally dreamed. He normally just closed his eyes and then when he opened them it was morning, plain and simple. This night he closed his eyes and as blissful relaxation loosened his muscles he was aware of something odd.

He was no longer in his bedroom.

He was standing on a stage.

He frowned to himself and looked around. Yes, it was most definitely a stage; a scuffed wooden surface that had seen many people cross it over the years. There was no lighting and there was no audience. There were metal chairs set out in rows facing him, but they remained unoccupied. McMillan ran a hand over his chin and started.

His chin was smooth. Not just clean-shaven but totally smooth.

Then there was his hand. He held it up in front of his eyes and gawped at the straight, young fingers. Not a touch of curve to them whatsoever.

"Well, I'll be..." he whispered as recognition of his location started to seep into his memory. He stared out over the chairs in front of him. Yes, there were the yellow lines marking a netball court. There were the dinner tables stacked in the corner. There over in the far corner was the entrance to the canteen. This was his old high school.

"Most peculiar," the young McMillan muttered to himself before he realised something else.

He could hear a noise.

Click click.

His head darted left and right. What was that?

Click click.

There it was again. Slightly nearer.

Click click.

It was coming from offstage, behind the black, voluminous curtains that ran from ceiling to floor. The youth stood transfixed, not breathing, as the sound came closer still.

Click...

click.

McMillan woke with a shriek and a start, his twisted hand grasping at his chest as he sat bolt upright in bed. Panting heavily he scanned the room for any sign of the clicking noise but saw none.

"Stupid. Stupid. Just a dream," he grumbled and swung his legs out of bed only to jump as he felt his right foot come down on something hard. When he had decided that his heart was not going to erupt out of his chest he lay chest down on the bed and leant over the side to investigate.

He came face to face with a ginning set of teeth.

"How the...?" McMillan pulled himself off the bed, grunted with the effort that bending down required and scooped up the old dentures. "I must be getting senile. I could have sworn I..." He shook his head, walked over to the dressing table and dropped the teeth into the small, circular bin that sat next to the piece of furniture before returning to bed, closing his eyes and...

standing once more on the school stage.

"Damn it!" the young McMillan swore as he quickly surveyed his surroundings. Still the same: old stage, empty chairs, all on his own.

And the noise just offstage.

Click click.

That was it! He had put up with too much. It was time for answers. McMillan stormed over to the curtains at the edge of the stage and pulled them open.

Click click.

There was the noise, but no source. It was coming from further backstage. Carefully, he picked his way through the dark, making sure not to trip over any discarded props or random pieces of PE equipment.

Click click.

It was here, in the dark. The noise was just in front of him, goading him, teasing him onwards. He would find it and choke some answers out of it. He was Howard Mc-Millan, a force to be reckoned with in the boardroom, a surging wave that swept through the business world and claimed all that lay before him. He would not be scared by the tiniest of noises in the dim recess of a puerile dream.

Click click.

There it was, to his side. He was right on top of it. So close now.

"Show yourself!" his young voice yelled into the dark.

Click click came the reply.

That was even closer. It was right next to him. Mc-Millan looked down and saw something scurry in the half-light, a flash of movement.

Click click.

Now it was on the opposite side and sounding faster. He spun to face it when something small and fast darted out of the gloom and placed a wooden hand...

on his chest!

There was something on his chest!

McMillan screamed himself awake and threw back the covers. There was a clatter as something small and hard tumbled to the floor. He darted around the bed and gaped in horror at what lay there grinning up at him.

"No." His voice was a tremulous gasp. "No, no, no." He lowered himself down and poked at the dentures. They just rolled over at his touch: inanimate, unthreatening.

The old man slumped onto the bed. Was he losing his mind? Twice now he had thrown them away and twice they had come back. This was not possible.

Then there was the dream. What the hell was that about?

Sleepwalking. Yes, that was it. He was suffering from the after-effects of anaesthetic and was sleepwalking when he was dreaming. He had gone over to the bins, picked up the dentures and carried them back in here whilst he had been asleep. That was the explanation.

The rational one, anyway.

He picked up the dentures and tossed them over to the bin where they dropped in with a satisfying rattle. Then he sat there, on the bed, and stared at the bin daring the discarded teeth to climb their way out.

They did not.

McMillan went back to bed.

He tucked himself up and left the light on. The clock radio said that it was 3:05 in the morning. Its red digits glowed dimly as he watched the numbers change.

3:06.

3:07.

3:10.

What? He sat upright and rubbed his eyes. He must have nodded off. That was okay. There had been no dream. He looked warily over to the dressing table, steeled up his nerve and got out of bed. Carefully he edged his way across the bedroom until his eye-line was level with the rim of the bin. He took a deep breath and peered in.

The teeth grinned back up at him from its depths.

McMillan nodded slowly to himself, reassured and made his way back to bed. He settled himself down, closed his eyes and...

looked out at the empty chairs.

"Oh no."

Click click.

"Oh no." His young Adam's apple bobbed nervously as he swallowed. This was not good. He had to escape. He had to get out of there. He darted to the edge of the stage and braked to a halt, his arms pinwheeling behind him.

This was not right. This was not how it was sup-posed to be. The drop from the front of the stage was not just high, it was *unbelievably* high. Nausea rose in his throat as vertigo caused his head to spin. It was like looking off a cliff edge and yet the chairs still sat there as if just a few feet away.

He could not escape that way.

Which meant only one thing.

Click click.

He would have to confront whatever it was that was hunting him.

McMillan faced the rear of the stage and shouted out, "Come on then! Show yourself! I'm not scared!"

Click click.

Closer.

Click click.

Closer still.

There was a flutter at the curtains and... was that a foot? A small, wooden foot?

Click click.

McMillan felt his throat dry up at the sight of the foot. An image from his distant past started to rise from the murk of his ancient memory as the foot was joined by a small wooden leg.

Click click.

McMillan started to back up. He was not in a very happy place right now. It was seventy-five years ago and his parents had laid on a treat for his fifth birthday. All his friends had been invited to the party and an entertainer had been hired.

Click click.

A puppeteer.

McMillan watched in horror as the curtains parted and the diminutive figure stepped forward.

Click click.

He had peed his trousers. There in front of all his friends, little Howie McMillan had voided his bladder down his legs because of one thing.

Click click.

The puppet grinned at him with painted lips and glossy teeth as it stalked robotically across the stage. It was a grin that had never known a human soul. It was without mirth or humour. It was a grin that said, "I'm coming for you. Not now, not soon, but one night when you least expect it I will creep up on you from the shadows and kill you where you sleep."

Click click.

Little Howie had turned and bolted out of the living room, screaming and wailing all the way to his bedroom where he had barricaded himself until that evening when his distraught mother had finally coaxed him out and persuaded him to take a long, warm bath to remove the reek of piss from his legs and the smears of snot and tears from his face.

Teenage Howard's fear grabbed his legs and turned them to run and he fled, hurling himself off the side of the cliff-like stage. The floor, many many meters below hit him like a speeding truck.

Imagine if you can this scene, a quiet house in a peaceful country lane. Walk through this house and listen to the stillness as you admire the objets d'art that its owner has acquired over the years; testaments to his success as a forthright and no-nonsense businessman.

Then, if you feel you can, if you feel you are not intruding, wend your way upstairs. Do not worry about making any noise, for there is no one here for you to disturb. Make your way along the landing, past the open bathroom door where the highly polished mirror reflects your look of curiosity and fear of being caught trespassing, then on to the main bedroom. Gently open the door and peer around its wooden protection before studying the sight inside.

You will see an old man lying still in bed. There is not a sound, not a murmur, not a snore as you tiptoe inside. You see a small waste bin lying empty on its side next to the dressing table and, as you pull back the curtains to allow some light into this place of rest, you can't help but see the red stains blooming out on the bedding which has been pulled up tight around his neck by his stiff, claw-like hands; bedding which has been drawn up in an involuntary act of self-protection and preservation.

As you step forward for a closer inspection, something grates under your shoe. You peer down and see that it is a tooth of sorts. In fact, it is not alone. There are a number lying discarded on the floor and across the bed-sheets. Picking some up you examine them and see that they are not real teeth, but replicas fashioned to the highest standards by an expert craftsman.

"But how can this be?" you ask yourself, for the man in bed is grinning in the light of the growing dawn. His lips are drawn back in a cruel rictus and there for you and all the world to see are a lopsided, ill-fitting pair of dentures. You frown when you realise that the tips of the false teeth are chipped and jagged as if they have been biting at something exceptionally hard.

Quietly you lay the fragments of implants down on the bed and unconsciously wipe your fingers against your shirt as you realise that you really should be leaving right about now.

Extraction

Harrison charged headlong, alarms echoing through the sterile corridors. He'd trained for this moment. Where potentially lethal substances were tested, every eventuality had to be considered.

The slightest slip by any of the facility's scientists could mean disaster, hence requiring skilled backup personnel.

He crashed into the sterile laboratory and was confronted with terrified faces.

Following their gaze, he instinctively swept up an idle beaker, flew across the room and upended it on the crawling, eight-legged miscreant.

As he left, hand firmly in place, he contemplated that his employers really ought to make sure their staff were not arachnophobes.

53, Bell Court

The wheels of the pushbike were a blur in the early evening twilight. The boy was pedalling furiously, conscious of the fact that the battery in his front light was dead and soon the street lights would be flickering into life. He had to finish the paper round before darkness set in or his dad would kill him for going out with dodgy lights. The rear one bracketed beneath his seat was fine. It glowed bright red and could be seen easily by cars. The front one though was deader than he would be in thirty minutes if he did not get a move on.

With a fresh push, he bumped up onto the footpath and cut across damp grass leaving a furrowed parting in his wake. His eyes darted left and right, making sure that he had not been seen. The last thing that he needed right now was some old biddy taking him to task for being a young hooligan with no regard for his elders. All he wanted to do was get the final three papers delivered and get home.

With a screech of brakes and an awesome sideways skid, he brought the bike to rest at the corner of a complex of small blocks of flats that were his next location: Bell Court. He hopped off and pushed the bike through the middle of the quad. Flowers grew in neat rectangular beds, some sort of fancy tree stood off to one side under which a cat dozed lazily.

A scene of peaceful tranquillity.

The boy shuddered and felt sick inside.

He rested his bike against a full-length glass window next to the door of one of the blocks of flats. "50 - 60 Bell Court," announced the sign stuck to the glass. The boy took a deep breath which was immediately followed by a sigh of the damned. He placed his hand on the door handle, turned and pushed. The intense smell of flowers wafted over him. He wriggled his nose which was fighting against the overwhelming fragrance of lavender and rose that made up the astringent air freshener someone had been spraying around down here. His trainers squeaked against the highly polished floor and he wondered how it was that the old people didn't slip over and break a hip or something. That was what old people did, wasn't it? They were feeble and frail which is why they ended up in places like this all penned together to keep them safe from harm. Well, that's what his mum said. She had told him that being old was a terrible thing. Your body started to shrivel and die once you hit sixty. Bits started to stop working properly and sometimes things even fell off! His gran had ended up in an old folks' home. They had gone to visit, just the once. Never again! It had been awful: the smell of wee, the muttering and ramblings of old crazy people, the sloppy food that dribbled down their chins...

The boy grimaced. No, he did not want to get old. He didn't know how, but he was going to cheat the ageing process. Somehow he was going to stay young and fit, just as he was now. Perhaps he could meet a vampire. A good one, mind; not an evil one. He could get the good vampire to turn him and keep him young. That would be cool. Okay, so he couldn't go out in the daytime, but surely living forever would be worth it.

Sometimes you just had to make a sacrifice. When people wanted to be doctors, they studied really hard and did not continually play computer games, which were a well-known distraction. Well, avoiding sunlight would be like that. It would be his sacrifice for living forever.

The boy gave a glance over his shoulder to make sure that his bike hadn't slipped down the glass window. It had done that once before and the handlebars had twisted. That had been a pain to fix. It was still stood propped up so he walked over to the foot of the staircase that led to the upper level.

It was dark up there.

It was *always* dark up there.

The boy pushed the light switch. It was one of those timer ones that popped back out after five minutes and the light went out to save electricity. The light at the top of the stairs flickered into life.

Five minutes. That was all he had. Easy. Run up the stairs, get the paper out of the bag, shove it in the flap and run like hell.

His feet were frozen at the foot of the stairs and the seconds ticked by.

The boy chewed at his bottom lip. This was silly, really silly. He reached into his bright yellow delivery bag and fished out a copy of the Chronicle. He folded it in four and tapped it against his left hand like a man weighing the chances he had of crossing a road of speeding traffic.

He glanced at the light switch, it was already starting to push back out. He was wasting time here. He had to deliver this paper then two more before legging it back home before dark. Slowly, he made his way up the staircase willing his legs to move, refusing to let them turn and run back down to the safety of the ground floor. With each step, his resolve was put under greater pressure. With each footfall, his knees trembled and his bladder ached until he finally stood at the top of the stairs.

He took a deep breath to steady himself and instantly gagged. Whereas the downstairs had smelt of chemically induced sprays of flowers, upstairs just smelt wrong. There was a dank mustiness in the air combined with a pervasive odour that normally accompanied something having been left in the fridge for far too long. He snapped his mouth shut, held his breath and pressed on along the corridor.

His destination was down the far end: number 53. The yellow door faced him, its glass panels staring at him out of the gloom. The light bulb was still out down there; it had been as long as he had been delivering papers on this round. Weren't they supposed to get fixed by a caretaker or someone? Surely the people living here must pay someone to do stuff like that, yet it never got fixed. Perhaps the caretaker didn't come up here. Perhaps the caretaker knew what was living in number 53.

A monster.

The boy swallowed as the word stomped into his thoughts. A monster lived there, behind the door that would have once been a bright yellow but was now a dull, fading shade of cream. It was as if the door itself had given up the ghost and died just like the plants. He looked at the dried, shrivelled up pot plants that sat next to the dead door. Like the faulty light, they too had never been tended to. They had just been left discarded.

The boy realised that his lungs were burning. He snatched a quick breath and grimaced at the foetid stench. It was even worse here as he got closer to the door. What was causing it?

The monster. That was what.

A creature lived in that flat that was so vile it had to cower in the dark away from prying eyes. It had created an evil lair where it pondered upon evil machinations. The boy had no idea what machinations were but he knew that's what monsters pondered on, whatever pondering was.

He was just a couple of footsteps away from the door now, the Chronicle grasped in his left hand like a trusty sword, albeit that trusty swords did not tremble quite so much. His eyes were fixed on the tattered net curtains that draped down behind the smudged glass windows of the door. They were brown and ragged. They didn't have the look of material that had been ripped apart. Instead, they looked as if they were simply falling apart, rotting where they hung. He edged closer, his eyes never leaving them. With every centimetre of approach and every move of each muscle he expected them to swish back and the monster to slam its ugly face up against the window. There would be fangs and teeth and fangs and more teeth. It would gnash and snarl at him as its slimy drool splattered against the grimy glass and its claws would scrape against the door in this dark recess of the corridor.

Closer still he edged. Closer and closer, his heart thrashing against his rib cage and his lungs screaming at his mouth to send them some air.

Eventually, he reached about fifty centimetres from the door and bent over to tease at the letter flap with his fingers. Slowly he lifted the flap, carefully checking to make sure nothing was peering out: no eyes, no antennae, no tentacles. When he was sure that the coast was clear he presented the newspaper to the slot and tapped it in. He didn't hear the thud of it falling to the floor on the other side as the sound of his running feet were making too much noise whilst conveying him out of the darkness and into the cool light of reality, the humdrum and the everyday.

As the boy fled down the corridor the decaying curtain twitched. A deformed hand withered with incredible age pulled the fraying material back and a haggard face loomed out of the murk. The pallid skin contrasted with the red-rimmed eyes, eyes filled with hunger.

This time, as many times before, it had been too slow. The ageing process was catching up with it. It needed to feed soon to maintain its longevity or it would waste away into old age and nothingness. That could not be allowed.

It would be young again with fresh blood coursing through its veins, then it would move on once more away from this dark little recess of a pathetic world where people just regarded its kind as bogeymen – stories with which to scare their children.

It would feed soon.

Perhaps tomorrow, when the newspaper came.

It would be waiting. Hungrily.

Needs Must

It was a nice well: roomy, dank and dark. There was just a glimmer of hurtful sunlight from the small aperture high above. This suited Odd Bod, suited him fine. As he sat in the noxious gloop that constituted the well's floor he scratched the infrequent tufts of hair on his scabrous scalp and decided that, overall, life had been very good to him. He had a safe place to live and there had been no hordes of angry villagers chasing him with pitchforks or other horticultural accoutrements.

The food, however, was becoming a problem.

Odd Bod tugged at a small bone that was lodged in the sticky floor and it parted company from the clinging substance with a wet *pop*. He blew at it and a piece of green slime dripped onto his knee. Absentmindedly rubbing at the slime with one hand, his other used the bone as an impromptu toothpick between his blackened incisors whilst he contemplated the issue of supplies.

There used to be plenty of food. It would come to the well, drop the wooden thing down to scoop up the wet stuff and, if he was hungry, Odd Bod would give the wooden thing a big tug causing the food to come crashing down into his waiting lap. True, it was a noisy experience when the food fell and sometimes it needed convincing that it really was food but, on the whole, it worked to Odd Bod's satisfaction.

Recently though the food had stopped dropping the wooden thing down. Odd Bod thought that this must be down to one of two reasons. It was either because the horrid wet stuff that the wooden thing used to scoop up had finally vanished or, and this possibility troubled Odd Bod more, that he had eaten all the food and there was none left.

Yes, that troubled Odd Bod a great deal. The thought of a world with no food was not a pleasant prospect at all even if he did live in a very nice dark, dank well with very little sunlight.

He hoped that it was the lack of the wet stuff that had caused the food to go away, he truly did because if the wet stuff came back then the food would, too. If, however, he had eaten all the food...

Odd Bod sadly shook his head. He had never been a fan of the wet stuff. It had always gotten everywhere and had made him feel as icky as the wet stuff itself. Odd Bod had fashioned himself small ledges between the crumbling bricks which had provided places for him to perch on when the wet stuff had risen up at certain times of the year. Then over the last few years the wet stuff had stopped rising. Instead, it had gotten lower and lower until all that was left was the gloop and the bits of broken bone that Odd Bod had discarded during his time in the well.

Odd Bod liked the gloop. It stuck nicely to his bony fingers and made his nose wrinkle when he sniffed it. Much more pleasant than the wet stuff.

However, if the wet stuff going away had caused

his food to disappear then that was a bad thing, whether Odd Bod liked the wet stuff or not, and something had to be done about it. The melancholy creature looked up to the small hole high above and sighed. There was only one way to find out what had happened to his food. Had it gone away or had it all been eaten? He had to find out or he would starve. It would not be the easiest of jobs, but one that had to be undertaken, nonetheless. His stomach rumbled and he whimpered disconsolately, his shaggy whiskers quivering around his mouth.

Odd Bod transferred the small bone from his hand to between his freshly picked teeth and placed a bare foot onto the lowest of the perches. He reached up with his hands - his cracked and broken nails searching out the tiniest of nooks and crannies with which to heave himself up. A foot edged up to another perch and his hands started to seek out more holes where he could cling securely between the bricks. After he had reached the same number of perches as he had fingers on his left hand he had to start work with the bone. Whilst clinging on with one set of fingers, the others used the bone to dig out handholds and footholds for him to utilise.

So it went on, time after time, transferring his weight onto newly excavated holes whilst digging out more and more spaces for his hands and feet. As he ascended the side of the well Odd Bod realised that the work was becoming harder and harder. Down below, the wall had been soft and easier to excavate. Up higher, it was tough and the bricks were much more firmly cemented together, but Odd Bod knew there could be no turning back. He peered down between his legs at his comfortable home and whimpered plaintively. What he would give to be settled down there once more with some fresh food, happily enjoying the knobbly, gristly bits that spurted goo all down his front as his teeth chomped into them. Instead, his muscles ached and his throat was dry. Moreover, to make matters worse, he was starting to feel very warm.

Odd Bod looked up and saw the reason for the increased heat: the hole at the top of the well was getting much larger! He had thought it was starting to increase in width when he had reached about halfway but he had dismissed the notion as silliness. Now, however, here he was, much higher up and the round hole was definitely letting in more of the hated sunlight. Odd Bod blinked as the brightness hurt his eyes and he focussed yet again on the task at hand, digging furiously between two stubborn bricks. Even the bricks seemed to be suffering from the sunshine. Down below, they had been beautifully dark and shiny; up here, they were dry and much paler in colour. Odd Bod shuddered as he dreaded what the evil sunshine would do to him when he eventually emerged from the well.

He carried on climbing.

In time, his breathing became somewhat laboured as his throat felt parched. Odd Bod started to whimper as he began to fear that he was not going to make it to the top of the well. Despair started to wash over him.

What if he slipped and fell? Would he make the same noises that the food normally made when it jumped down to him?

What if he got to the top and discovered that he had eaten all the food? His stomach roared and he shook his head. No, he must not think such things. Food had to be out there. It had just gone away when the wet stuff had disappeared!

He glanced up and squeaked in both fear and excitement. Fear because the hole was now so wide that he could not see all the way around it. Excitement because he was only about an arm's length from the top. A broad grin of blackened teeth spread across his face and he clambered towards the rim of the well.

Odd Bod's stomach lurched as his foot slipped and his arm swung free. Screaming loudly he gripped with one hand on the bone that was currently dug between two bricks.

Silly Odd Bod!

Silly Odd Bod!

He had let his excitement get the better of him and had lost his concentration. With one firm tug on the bone, he swung his loose arm up and grabbed at the tiniest of gaps in the unforgiving brickwork. His nails prised themselves in and he hissed in pain as the rough surface dug into his grey flesh. Desperately, his feet scrambled at the sheer wall below him, propelling his weight up towards the rim of the well. He discarded the bone, ignoring the tool as it tumbled down towards the dark, comforting gloop. Instead, he hauled his hand up to the precipice above him. His fingers flailed around crumbling material on the rim until they found sound purchase and the rest of his withered body scurried up the last little distance. With one, firm lunge he heaved himself up and over the edge of the well. He rolled head over heels and landed with a thump on something that was most definitely not gloop.

Odd Bod bent over onto all fours and peered closely at the stuff. It covered the floor around the well. It felt strange to his gloop-accustomed touch and consisted of a multitude of little strands of near-identical material that stood together in the near vicinity.

He sniffed it. It wobbled as he did so.

Carefully he picked some out and stuck it in his mouth before chewing.

"Pah!" He spat the disgusting substance out and wiped spittle from his face with the back of his dirt-encrusted hand.

"Why are you eating grass?"

Odd Bod's head snapped up and his eyes located the source of the noise. It was food; a small morsel, but food nonetheless. He grinned.

The food giggled as it clasped its hands over its mouth. "You look funny," it laughed.

Odd Bod sat down on the horrid-tasting stuff and scratched his threadbare scalp. This food was strange. Food normally made noises like, "Oh, God! No! No!" or "Please no! I have children!" This one sounded different. In addition, it was not covered in delicious icky stuff.

He pointed with a chipped and broken fingernail. "Food?" his gravelly voice enquired.

"Sure," said the little red-haired girl. "I've got lots. Teddy and I are having a tea party on the blanket over there."

Odd Bod's eyes followed her small finger as it pointed over to a small furry thing that sat on the thing called a *blanket*. "Food?" he asked again.

The little girl walked over to him and took his warty hand in hers. "Come on. We have plenty."

Odd Bod clambered to his feet and slowly lurched along behind her as she led him over to the blanket where the small, inanimate furry thing was propped up against a grey stone. In front of it were a number of round receptacles of different sizes along with an object that had a handle on one side and a pointy bit on the other. The girl patted the blanket next to her and Odd Bod seated himself down, tucking his gangly legs beneath him. He frowned as his brain used to years of peaceful solitude tried to make sense of the situation. As his grey cells bumped together in confusion, the little girl handed him one of the round things. "Here you go," she said. "Cake."

The very perplexed diner took the object in both his hands and stared at it. It was flat and about the size of one of his hands. It was decorated around the edge with pink flowers. Not sure what to do, he shoved it in his mouth and started to chew.

"No!" exclaimed the girl, leaning over and dragging the thing out of his mouth. "Don't eat the plate. Eat the cake." She proceeded to hold her own plate and seemingly feasted on thin air.

Odd Bod did likewise. The air did not taste of anything. He frowned.

"It is only *make-believe*, you know," the girl whispered into his ear. "There isn't really any cake. Just don't tell Teddy. He'll get upset."

Odd Bod looked over at Teddy. The small, furry thing was making no apparent effort to eat the make-believe cake. Whatever cake was. Odd Bod sighed and glanced longingly over his shoulder to his well.

"Are you thirsty?"

"Thirsty?" Odd Bod asked.

The girl was now placing a different receptacle in front of him. This one was also decorated in flowers but was somewhat deeper in shape. "I'll pour some nice tea in the cups." She picked up the odd-looking thing with the handle and poured a clear liquid into the cups before offering one to her guest. "Here you go."

Odd Bod took the little cup awkwardly in his misshapen fingers and raised it to his mouth. His nose caught a whiff of its smell and wrinkled in disgust. He snapped his head back and grimaced.

"Now, don't be rude," the little redhead scowled. "Drink it all up."

Odd Bod looked across the rim of the cup to this strange piece of food that was not acting as it should then peered down into the cup unsure as to what he should do. Part of him wanted to reach over and gobble her up but part of him felt he really ought to do as he was told. It was only polite.

He placed the cup to his lips.

The girl smiled and nodded for him to continue. "Down in one," she said.

Odd Bod did as he was instructed and gulped the liquid down.

He immediately regretted the decision.

Emily carefully tidied up the blanket and the tea set. She cautiously poured the remains of the so-called *tea* down the dry, foul-smelling well - the well in which her mummy had died. She had no idea what she had put in the teapot but it seemed to have done the trick. It had been a concoction of all sorts of liquids from tins in the cellar, the labels of which had borne loud warning symbols.

It had worked a treat.

She had been terribly scared when the monster had climbed out of the well, but it had saved her the job of climbing down to do what had needed doing. Besides, Teddy had been there for moral support.

The thing that had eaten her mummy and so many other villagers lay dead at her feet.

She bundled Teddy and the tea set into the blanket, swung the improvised bag over her shoulder and skipped merrily home.

Just Like Everybody Else

So, have you ever wanted to kill someone?

Now, I don't mean that silly little thing where you get mad at some idiot who cuts you up on the motorway and you shout out, "Oh, I could kill you, darn it!" No, not that. Nor when your loved one has let you down at the last minute for some romantic soirée or some such and you say, "Wait till I get my hands on him..." and so on, and so on.

No, I don't mean that at all.

That's not really wanting to kill someone, is it? That's just getting a bit ticked off when you feel rather annoyed. You crease your brow, thump your fists onto your hips and just vent whatever comes into your mouth. There might be some choice language, some expletives, other such stuff and then you say that you want to kill someone.

You don't *really* want to kill them. You want to *punish* them but right there and then you are so miffed that you can't think of the appropriate retribution to inflict so you just say that you want to kill them.

That's not what I mean at all.

I mean, have you ever really wanted to *kill*

someone? Have you wanted to extinguish their light, snuff out their candle or obliterate any other such twee cliché that we use when we say that someone has been removed from mortal existence?

That sort of kill someone.

Of course you have.

We all have.

Don't deny it. I can tell. You're blushing, so it must be true. You're sitting there, reading this and shifting uncomfortably in your seat. Perhaps you're on the bus, riding to work next to that guy who never bathes or you're curled up in bed with your loved one as they softly snore themselves to sleep? You could be anywhere, but right now you're thinking to yourself: *How does he know?*

Well, the answer to that is simple.

We all want to do it at some point in our life. After all, it's only human.

We all have *urges*.

Sure, there are the urges that we will happily talk about to friends and family: we get hungry, we get tired, we feel horny. These are all socially acceptable to a certain degree, but that same society frowns so deeply on the one urge that constantly niggles away at the back of our heads.

The need to kill.

I wonder why that is?

If it's there, it must be perfectly natural, surely? If it wasn't then evolution would have stripped it from us the moment we jumped down from the trees and started wandering around on two feet. Perhaps it's some archaic psychological trauma, founded from when we were prey and watched our loved ones being feasted upon by those wild monsters further up the primal food chain? Perhaps it's our need for dominance over those around us to ensure that our seed continues to thrive?

Perhaps.

I'm not convinced though.

I'm more inclined to think it's our brain doing a bit of judicial weeding of society. Let's face it, we all have our own ideas as to what is right and what is wrong. Surely we want to see those personal norms spread through our community and the wider world? What's a more effective way of making sure that those values survive than removing those individuals that oppose them? We see it all the time at the international level. Governments sanction the deaths of those who stand against them either through war, assassination or execution, so what's to stop us from doing it at a somewhat lower level?

You, on the bus: the guy next to you who always smells and hasn't seen a bath for an eternity - he repulses you, doesn't he? Follow him one day and get rid of him. One less smelly guy.

You, with the snoring partner. What do you think pillows were *really* invented for?

Try it.

It's liberating.

Anyway, I'm rambling here. Where was I?

Oh, yes. Urges.

We all have them, but what's the best way to follow them through?

"Well, I could get myself a gun and blow someone's head off," I hear you cry. Really? You think it's that simple? Sure, if you want to get caught! Don't you ever watch CSI? Police are quite clever these days; they use science. Everyone knows that each gun has its own *fingerprint*. The bullet leaves the barrel at a certain speed or angle and can be quickly matched to a specific gun. No, if you use a gun then your killing will have been in vain. They'll catch you, lock you up and throw away the key.

And don't get me started on strangling. Go ahead, compress someone's carotid artery and see how far *that* gets you. There's bound to be fingerprints, some trace of fabric or your DNA under the victim's fingernails as they fight frantically for their life. No, you strangle someone you might as well walk into a police station with a large cardboard sign around your neck saying, "I did it!"

Poison? So you're a trained chemist now, are you? Jesus! Have you looked at all those potential victims around you? Are they all the same size? Do they all have the same metabolism? Not a chance; far too risky. You could slip them a Mickey, sit back and watch them just get incredibly giggly. Now wouldn't *that* be annoying? Worse still, you might achieve a less than half-decent job and they could come staggering at you across the room gagging and frothing at the mouth as they try to rip your eyes out. Not a pretty sight, I'm telling you.

No. There is only one, sure-fire way to kill someone.

A knife.

Small, sharp and thrust quickly in the side. Make sure you hit a major organ or rummage around so much that they bleed out rapidly. Okay, it's messy. Not a method you'd want to do on your favourite Persian rug, I agree, but it's effective.

It's also satisfying, the feeling of their life gently ebbing away as you cradle them in your arms.

Blissful.

For the ones you like, that is.

The ones you hate? Just slit their wretched necks

and be done with it. Probably best standing on a bridge at the time so you can push them into the water and watch them drown bloodily. Very gratifying.

Ah, the very thought of it; taking someone who you want removed and dispatching them quickly and efficiently.

Yes! There you go. That little glint in your eye and the quick intake of breath. You saw it, didn't you? Just for a second. You saw the look on their face when you plunged the blade in: the shock, the confusion. You felt the rush of satisfaction: the total, utter glee. It won't leave you now. It's there, imprinted on your retinas. Perhaps they throw their head back slightly in pain as you witness a stretched artery pumping futilely while their blood gushes from their wound onto the floor? Yes, perhaps.

You're licking your lips and you don't know why. You're not hungry for food, but you crave something else.

Something deeper.

Something insatiable.

Now you know what I mean. Now you hear what I'm saying.

You're just like everybody else. You're just like me and I'm just like you. The question is, "What are you going to do about it?"

I know what *I'm* going to do. The only question is, *to whom*?

Perhaps it might be you?

Second Time Around

The bar stank of warm beer, hormonal sweat and stale urine. These were not aromas that pleased the smartly dressed woman who resided in a corner booth whilst she nursed a poorly made cocktail. Her preferences lingered more in the exotic: drifting incense, burning coals and sweet perfumes. The fragrances of devotion, not boredom.

A smile touched her perfectly glossed lips as she remembered better times and she played idly with the artificially coloured red cherry which was impaled on a cheap cocktail stick. A droplet of her feeble excuse for a drink rolled down the fruit's surface and dripped towards the table. The woman frowned and the alcohol hovered in mid-air, never reaching the sticky woodwork. Slowly, it defied all laws of gravity and rose upwards before starting to spin ferociously, gaining momentum. The woman stared intently at the droplet, watching the dim lights of the student bar flicker in its surface before pointing a slender, manicured finger at the liquid and sending it hurtling across the room.

A young male clasped his hand to the back of his

neck and turned around, glowering with anger as he tried to spot who had just flicked something at him. His eyes found the woman and she smiled at him, knowingly.

He smiled back.

She drained her drink, rose gracefully from her seat and walked past the young man as she exited the bar. He trailed obediently behind. The woman smiled as she scented a new aroma on the air.

Desire.

Slowly, she walked her way down the covered pathway of the urban campus, her red heels clicking enticingly on the paving slabs as they encouraged the young man to keep up. As she turned a corner she paused and watched him staggering hungrily behind her. She needed no beckoning gesture, no *come-hither*. He was her's, utterly and completely.

The alley down which she walked darkened as the overhead lighting became more infrequent. This was a forgotten area where staff and students rarely ventured; a dead spot on the campus. The woman arrived at a place where a rusting door hung askance from its frame. Not wanting to damage her perfect nails, the woman extended her hand and a thin stream of water extruded from her fingertips. It pressed against the old door and forced it open, allowing her unhindered access.

The young man followed her into the dark storeroom. "I'm yours," he whispered hoarsely.

"I know," came a deeply sensual voice in reply. "You always have been. You always will be." Her manicured fingers ran up his chest and around his neck, drawing him close. The man gasped as she latched his mouth onto hers.

He kissed her wildly.

She let him.

His hands ran over her back and through her hair.

She thought about legions of worshippers bowing down before her under an excruciatingly hot sun.

His fingers ran up her front and found her soft breast.

She remembered the smell of blood and entrails spewing from those sacrificed solely for her amusement.

He started to gag and splutter. The woman's fingers gripped his head tight and locked his mouth against hers. Water trickled slowly from the seal of their lips.

The man's eyes flashed in terror and the last thing he saw was a pair of flames peering curiously at him.

Then there was blackness.

"Having fun?"

Asherah ignored the mocking male voice as she let her lip-gloss adjust itself whilst she stepped out of the storeroom.

"So what? You're just going to leave it there?"

Her locks of hair tidied themselves as she stopped, sighed and said, "You were late. I was bored."

There was the sound of footsteps and her interrogator stepped into view, the feeble light casting an unhealthy sheen to his sallow skin. "One of these days you'll get caught, and what will you do then?"

"Like you really care for my well-being. You're just concerned that I'll drag you down with me." She turned and carried on walking. He fell in step at her side. "So why were you late, as if I really care?"

"I've been shopping."

She eyed him up and down from the corner of her eye. His long, black coat almost touched the floor as he walked. "Can't see any difference. You still look like a reject from an Anne Rice novel."

Her companion reached into his coat, ignoring the insult. "Got myself this."

Asherah sighed again as she glanced briefly at the gleaming, brand new pistol. "What on Earth do you need that for? You can just *bore* people to death."

"I liked the look of it," he explained, pointing the gun at random pieces of stonework and glancing down the sight. "It goes with the image."

"Really, Asmodeus! Tell me for the umpteenth time, why did we leave Heaven?"

"Don't start on about that again."

"You're just one bright idea after another, aren't you?"

"It wasn't my fault! It was..."

Asherah flapped an annoyed hand at her fellow angel. "Don't say it! Don't mention his name. Don't *ever* mention *his* name. Remember the last time we crossed his path?"

Asmodeus nodded as he stowed the gun away. "Too well."

They walked on in contemplative silence until the female angel finally said, "I'm going to be uncontactable for a while. That's why I needed to see you."

"Oh? I thought you had a thing going on here? With that student."

"Malcolm?" Asherah nodded. "I did, but he's getting so intense. It's all *when are we going to destroy the world*? I've had enough. I'm going to ditch him tonight and head off on my own for a bit."

They were now walking back up to the main square of the campus. The bars had emptied and they were alone, all except for a lone figure sat on the steps at the far side of the square.

"That him?"

Asherah nodded.

"Good luck," Asmodeus said and slipped away leaving her on her own.

The former goddess of Canaan gave herself a quick mental check over and walked across the square to her last remaining disciple.

A puppy dog. A small, bouncy terrier that's so eager to please, Asherah thought as she climbed the staircase, her young disciple, Malcolm Wallace chattering away excitedly in front of her. "So, let me get this straight," she said out loud as they emerged onto the youth's corridor, "you persuaded your friends to recite an incantation which would bind a ghost to the physical realm?"

Wallace nodded, his strange orange pupils bouncing up and down with delight. "Sam fell for it completely."

"How?"

"He's desperate to know what's going to happen to his terminally ill father when he dies."

Asherah paused and ran a polished nail against Wallace's cheek. "That's *terribly* wicked. I *like* it." She thought Wallace was going to faint with joy right there. She would give him five minutes, see what he had to show her then kill him before heading off into the night with whatever she felt like from his personal stash of paraphernalia.

"Are they in there?" She nodded over Wallace's shoulder to the glass door leading into what appeared to be a kitchen. She could make out two figures slumped over a table.

Wallace nodded again, turned, looked in the kitchen then his face fell. Asherah immediately realised what was wrong. His friends were alone.

"No ghosty," she whispered and pushed past into the room, her heels clicking on the tiled floor. Slowly, she glanced around, not just with her eyes but with all her senses and intuition. The two fellow students seemed to be fast asleep, there was the unmistakable smell of beer in the air and there was an empty chair at the head of the table. As Asherah glided past the chair and let her fingers run along its back, she felt an unmistakable tingle shimmy up her spine causing her to smile. There *had* been something else here; something supernatural. Perhaps it had escaped or perhaps...

Perhaps these two youths had managed to rid themselves of it.

She looked from one to the other. One was slightly overweight, sporting a downy boy-beard and roaring louder than a bad-tempered dromedary. The other was of average height with a mop of curly hair and...

Asherah had to prevent herself from taking a sharp intake of breath. *Hello,* she thought. *What have we here?* Her heels continued to click purposefully as she circled the table and reached the curly-haired youth. There was something about him, something she could not quite pin down.

It intrigued her.

That certainly beat being bored.

She let her nails stroke up the boy's neck and into his hair causing him to groan slightly in his sleep. "This one's rather cute," she said over her shoulder as Wallace entered the room, a thundercloud rumbling above his head.

"They must have removed him before we got here," he grumbled as he wrote something down on a scrap of paper. "Shame. I would have liked to see the looks on their faces."

Asherah's manicured nails continued to play with the curly hair as she decided that she would like to see the look on the youth's face too. She started to hum a low tune under her breath. The boy gasped sharply in his slumber and she felt his body tense with arousal.

"Stop that!" Wallace hissed. "We don't have time."

Asherah ceased her little tune and the boy settled back down to sleep. There was not enough time now, but there would be in the future, she decided. Perhaps Wallace could be of use to her after all? He could suit her needs and then, when his path crossed with this youth's again, she would jump ship and let her student sink ignominiously into the Abyss.

"Later," she whispered to the sleeping boy before stalking out of the room. Wallace shoved the piece of paper into his friend's hand and followed her down the stairwell. "Tell me, Malcolm," the goddess purred, "have I ever told you about The Divergence?" She turned to face her disciple and...

...stood outside watching Asmodeus slinking off into the shadows. "Good luck," he called over his shoulder.

Asherah spun on her heels, suddenly dizzy and confused. This was not right. This had already happened.

Along with a shed load of other things.

She remembered them happening.

With her long-time partner in crime gone, she turned and looked out once more into the square. Wallace was there again, but this time he was not alone. When the angel saw who was with him, she could not help but smile. "Well, *hello*," she grinned. "Fancy meeting you here," she murmured under her breath.

It was the curly-haired boy from the kitchen, but he had grown up and Asherah liked how he had grown. He oozed anger and hatred and...

"Apparently he can fly," she mused to herself as the man grabbed Wallace by the neck then jumped up to the top of the old chimney that adorned the corner of the square. Leaning against a pillar, Asherah beamed at the sound of her disciple screaming pitifully in the night. "Aww, *widdle baby*," she laughed, raising her hand to her mouth to stifle her chuckles. This was hilarious. She had not had so much fun since... Well, for a very long time, at least. Who was this stranger? He was intoxicating. He stood at the top of the chimney holding onto a writhing Wallace. "Let go, let go, let go," Asherah hissed, pounding a fist into her hand. "I want to see him fall."

She was not disappointed.

"Oh, that's gotta hurt," she jeered as her disciple smacked into the hard paving slabs. However, it was not over yet. The stranger jumped easily from the chimney top and glided down to the body of his victim. He stood there, looking down at Wallace drumming his fingers on his teeth before crouching down as if something was wrong.

Asherah gave a start when she saw the seemingly dead Wallace's hand shoot up and grab his assailant by the wrist. "Now, who's been doing extra homework?" she purred, her eyes bright with fire and glee. The two males went at it tooth and claw, pounding with fists and slapping with words until finally the stranger appeared to have the upper hand. Then, for the second time that night, Asherah felt truly amazed as she heard three non-words leave the stranger's mouth.

"…

"…

"…"

"How?" she gasped, truly shocked. "That's not possible. How could he?" The portal to Beyond flared open as she tried to work out how the stranger had learnt the incantation that Asmodeus had taught her and she had passed on to Wallace. They were the only three creatures in existence who knew how to do that.

Until now, apparently.

This was marvellous! She strode across the square, clapping slowly as she did. "Oh, well done. Well done indeed," she offered in congratulation as the victor looked over. A glimmer of recognition seemed to light his face as he glanced down at his prey then back up to her. She wandered idly over to some stone steps and settled herself down, stretching her legs out in front of her. "Well, go on then."

"Pardon?" The man's voice cracked as he spoke and a slight air of confusion swept across his face.

She pointed to the portal with a finely manicured finger. "Finish him off. I don't have all night and I've been so looking forward to this." Smiling her cruellest smile, she gave full reassurance that she was deadly serious.

The man's concentration had obviously been broken as Wallace rolled out from underneath him. "What do you mean?" her disciple whined. "You can't be serious!"

Asherah sighed. *Here we go*, she thought. *Mister Petulant.* She made as if she were studying her nails and changed the hue of their varnish a few times before look-ing up and saying, "Oh, are you still here? Not taken over the world yet? You know that gets so *dull* in the end. 'Look, look, here's the universe I destroyed for you!' Bor-ring." She turned her attention to the stranger. "I've had an eternity of that you know. It's okay the first few times, but it gets dull ever so quickly." The thing was, she real-ised, that she wholeheartedly meant it. Here she was, a fallen angel, doomed to walk amongst lesser beings who would become infatuated with her and promise her the world and its apocalypse over and over again. It was just so monotonous.

This guy, however...

Asherah smiled. He felt different. As he stood there breathing heavily, his eyes darting from her to Wallace then to the portal, he presented no signs that he needed to fall down and worship her, no desire to be a mindless minion.

He felt unique.

Unlike Wallace who was now snivelling and beg-ging her to let him live. "You can't do this," he whined. "We had plans."

"*You* had plans!" Asherah had had enough and she snapped at him like a serpent at a rodent. "I was just hav-ing fun and now I'm not. You're boring, Malcolm. So damned boring." She stood in one fluid motion. "I'm through with you. Finished."

"Please, please don't leave me." Good grief he was actually weeping now. Pitiful. "What will I do without you?"

Asherah looked up at the ball of hatred that stood behind her former disciple and, for a brief moment, she was no longer standing in a paved square of a small-town university. She saw the insides of a small cellar where an older version of Wallace stood gloating before sending an unfortunate teenage boy through the same portal that stood dangerously next to him in the here and now. Asherah nodded in realisation of what she had seen through the stranger's eyes. "Quite frankly, after what you are going to do to his son, I really don't think that's an issue. Goodbye, Malcolm."

With that, she turned and walked away, hiding the beaming grin on her face. Life was going to be so much more fun the second time around.

Humble Pie

"My word, this filling is most delicious," Charles said to his sister-in-law. "It's a shame Josh couldn't join us for dinner tonight."

"Did you say he was away on business?" the effusive banker's perfectly manicured wife asked their demure hostess.

Angela thoughtfully rubbed the angry bruise on her wrist. "I'm not sure when he'll be back."

"Ah, well. You must give us the recipe,"

The quiet woman smiled serenely as she recalled the slashing of the knife and the screaming of her erstwhile bullying husband. "I'm afraid I couldn't do that," she explained. "It's a family secret."

Relic

It was a moment of true wonder.

The sturdy chains creaked and the peering onlookers held their breath as the swaying crane tentatively eased the last remaining chunk of ancient detritus out of the archaeological pit. The patchwork of old stone and rubble wobbled like an uncertain octogenarian as it rose hesitantly into the expectant air before being gently lowered to the awaiting space at the side of the dig.

The site supervisor barged his way to the front of the rubbernecking crowd. He was normally a quiet man, content to just chip away at the layers of accumulated dust and dirt that had covered civilisation over the millennia of time, but today he was having to raise his voice to be heard. "Back! Back, I say! Everyone back! Let me through."

A reporter tried to push a camera into the squat, little man's face. The supervisor grabbed it by the lens and shoved hard causing the intruder to swear loudly. He had no time for any of these frivolities. He had work to do. This was the greatest find of the century and it needed cataloguing, preserving and studying. His breath came in short, hard gasps and his skin sweated profusely as he finally managed to elbow his way to the edge of the pit. "Well?" he shouted down.

About five metres down, two members of his team were busily brushing away dust and fragments of earth from the now exposed surface.

"Well?" the supervisor inquired again, his voice squeaking with agitated falsetto. "What's down there?"

One of the archaeologists looked up, beaming from under his protective hat. "It's amazing, Sir. Truly amazing."

And it was.

It took another month to extract the relic from the archaeological pit and what a month it was. The media hype had shot around the world like flame on gunpowder. All manner of theories had started to spring up as to what the item actually was: some thoughtful, some absurd. Such was the nature of humanity, the supervisor pondered as he regarded the thing of ancient beauty that lay in front of him under the temporary canvas roof of the site's mobile headquarters.

Tenderly he ran a callused finger along the rough edge of the artefact, smiling wistfully as he did so. It had been quite a struggle to extricate it from the pit. The relic had quite obviously been part of a larger construction at one point – there were jagged edges to some of the curious round stones that made up its main body – but something had caused it to fracture. Perhaps subsidence or geological pressures over the years had snapped the item into smaller pieces? The man shook his head at the wonder that there might be more of this curious object down under the earth: still buried, awaiting discovery.

His eyes travelled between the round, interlocking lattice of stone that rose and fell like a vast range of hills, a rolling countryside. Although the stones were similar in size and dimension – approximately ten centimetres across – they were by no means uniform. Some were slightly larger, some smaller. Was there a meaning to this? Was there a pattern here that he had yet to decipher? His trembling hand ran tremulously over his balding scalp. There were also small gaps between the stones as if there had been something there in times gone past that was now missing. He had theorised that organic matter had once dwelt there but had rotted away over the years. His team were still scouring every nook and cranny for evidence of wood, grass, seeds or any other material to verify this. It was indeed a painstaking job.

Then there was the script.

There was not much of it, but it was clear and evident for all to see. This was what had caused the excitement on the day of the excavation. It was brilliant white and scrolled its way across five of the stones.

It was causing a headache extraordinaire.

There was no record of this writing form in any of the extensive databases through which the supervisor and his team had searched. They had rooted through archive after archive trying to match this scrolling penmanship but there was nothing at all that was even a close match. It had them completely confounded. This was, to say the least, problematic. The *powers that be* had invested a huge amount of finance into this excavation and they demanded results. They were sending specialists over this afternoon to examine the script. Apparently, political pressure was being applied to the backers of the project and with times being what they were that meant someone's head could roll.

Or worse.

The supervisor regarded his timepiece. It was almost time for the so-called specialists to arrive. Would they be able to decipher the code or would they be just as stumped as he was? He was guessing the latter and that worried him greatly.

"As we can see from the way that this character here quite clearly links the two on either side, we can be sure that this is a call to the faithful visiting the shrine."

Heads bobbed up and down, intent on demonstrating sage wisdom when the brains contained within did not have the foggiest idea as to what the speaker was explaining.

The relic had been a resident at the Chatterton Institute for around five months now and had been subjected to every possible form of analysis that a league of esteemed academics could apply. The result was this weeklong symposium where the greatest minds hid their bafflement at what was still a total enigma. True, some of the fine academics got up and made very colourful descriptions about what they believed the artefact to be, but their surrounding peers knew better. It was all gibberish. The scientific community was at a complete dead end.

Other groups, though, had different ideas. There had been rumours circulating that idealistic factions wanted to take control of the artefact. They claimed that the scientists were, in fact, hiding something dark and insidious. Theories and speculative ideas had now started to surface from the more radical quarters of society. As a result, security at the symposium was tantamount.

However, one cannot inhibit a driven radical from

his or her purpose.

Rapid gunfire rattled through the hall and terrified scientists dove for cover as some guards fell to the floor dead whilst others unshouldered their arms and returned defensive fire. Canisters flew into the vast room and smoke started to snake its way out of the small cylinders. The guards and the scientists coughed and gagged as they gasped for air until in a few seconds they lay still and immobile.

Masked figures stalked their way through the smoke, wary in case anyone was playing possum. Their guns flicked left and right, nervously. When they were sure that they were the only living souls in the room, a giant of a man strode up to the artefact, regarded it from behind his mask as a one might look upon a beautiful predator, unsure whether to be in awe of its sleek design or terrified that it might snap its jaws around one's middle. Eventually, he nodded slowly and smiled behind his face-plate. He signalled for his men to come forward with chains and a gurney.

The relic belonged to them now. With it they would build a new tomorrow.

"Today sees the birth of a new world!"

The video footage was grainy, amateur. The camera shook as if it was not attached to a tripod but was instead held tightly by an overexcited disciple of the cause.

"We, and only we," continued the speaker, a tall man dressed head to toe in white, "know the truth to the mystical writing that was unearthed and stolen from public view by the Chatterton Institute. This," the camera zoomed in hastily on the artefact at which the speaker was pointing, "is a legacy from our past. It was inscribed by wise men who knew that we held our lives in our hands. It tells of days to come when the oppressed shall rise up and claim what is rightfully theirs. It was written..."

He never finished his sentence.

A shot rang out and a red dot appeared on his forehead as a look of disbelief took control of his facial muscles before he fell backwards to the floor.

The camera swung round to capture a squad of black-clad soldiers bursting into view. One raised his gun to the lens and then there was static.

"This cannot be permitted to continue."

The voice was calm and clipped but unbridled anger bubbled under the surface.

"No, Sir."

"We must claim the Chatterton Stones for ourselves, for our people."

"Yes, Sir."

From his luxurious seat behind his mammoth mahogany desk, the ruler of the most powerful country on the planet peered over steepled fingertips at his entourage of advisers. *Advisers*? They were anything but. They were just a bunch of fawning *Yes Men*: bringing him Cappuccinos, sorting his mail and agreeing with whatever he said. If he told them to go jump in the lake outside his office then they would do so gladly with beatific smiles on their faces.

And that was exactly what he wanted.

There was no room for advice nowadays. What was needed was vision and action, and right now he was going to act. "Is the task force ready?"

"Yes, sir."

He nodded. "Then send them in."

"It's no good, Sir. They have broken into the compound."

Another leader from another country looked out over another entourage of *Yes Men*. "The Chatterton Stones?"

The advisers looked cautiously from one to another. Terror bounced back and forth between their eyes as they mentally drew straws. Eventually, one poor soul lost. "They have been extracted by the hostiles." He cringed awaiting the wrath of his leader.

Instead, there was a pondering silence.

After what seemed like an hour but was in reality just a few seconds, the same adviser asked, "Sir, what do you want to do?"

The leader sat back in his swivel chair and stared out of the window. From this high up he could see most of the capital. Down there, men and women went to work, children played and innocents carried on with their everyday lives.

Lives that would be ruined if his country's enemies cracked the code that was scrawled across the Chatterton Stones.

He could not let that happen.

"Order a pre-emptive strike," he whispered, "and may God have mercy on our souls."

Before the first missile struck, a reciprocating flotilla of devastation had been launched in the opposite direction. The fire of jet propulsion burned up into the fragile atmosphere and guided the rockets to their doomed targets. All hit with deadly precision. The Earth's atmosphere was set aglow with the impacts. Mushroom clouds billowed up to the stratosphere, scorching the ground, poisoning the air and slaughtering millions in a matter of minutes.

There were inevitable repercussions. For too long the world had been teetering on the brink of oblivion. For millennia, the planet's inhabitants had borne the interminable load packed to the brim with grudges of hate and spite whilst sharpening their blades in silence. These acts of aggression from the highest levels unstopped the dams that had held back the flow of pent up hatred and homicide. Country turned on country, neighbour turned on neighbour, child turned on parent. Within a matter of days the entire planet was consuming itself in an orgy of bilious devastation. The population declined within weeks as its inhabitants bled to death in the deserted streets and the leaders of humanity were now impotent, unable to prevent the onslaught or turn back the raging waters of the dam that had been breached.

No one tended the fields.

No one fed the livestock.

Energy supplies became erratic and the sick were left to die.

Within a year the human race was a mere shadow of its former glory. It slunk off, found itself a dark hole in which to hide and there, pondering how all this could have come about over a collection of old stones covered in unintelligible writing, it curled up, closed its eyes and breathed its last.

"Damn it!"

Colin Gibson eased himself up from the kneeling position in front of his white Ford Cortina. He had completed the touch-up job underneath the bumper where the rust had been speckling through the paintwork, but he had managed to drip some of the white paint on the cobbles between the weeds that always seemed to poke their way up no matter what he threw at them.

He shook his head. He really should have used spray paint rather than the old tin of gloss he had found kicking around under the sink. The gloss covered the rust great but it was a pain to clean up.

He shrugged as he snapped the lid back on the tin.

Ah well. A bit of paint on some old cobbles was hardly a disaster was it?

Armitage

"Welcome, valued customer of Multinational Megabrand!" chirped the hologram of the pretty, blue-eyed brunette with the gentle hint of a Scottish accent. "We are pleased to inform you that your multi-purpose, sub-dermal, self-diagnosis device (version 5.5) is working at optimum capacity. As a result, it has diagnosed that you have a..."

"...*common cold...*" stated a flat, lifeless Home Counties male voice as the woman's lips moved ever so slightly out of sync.

"We have a hundred per cent cure rate for this illness, so," continued the perky female, back in time with her own words, "in no more than twenty standard minutes, a Multinational Megabrand patient service drone will arrive at your door in order to provide you with the relevant treatment. Please make sure that you are there to greet them. And don't forget to smile. Remember, a happy patient is a healthy patient.

"You have been charged fifty Megabucks for this message which will be taken from your personal savings account in twenty-four hours. If you do not pay within five minutes, the standard rate of sixteen point five per cent interest will be applied at an hourly rate."

The face of the hologram morphed briefly into a frolicking unicorn with *MM* stamped on its shiny white arse before dissolving into the back of Armitage's hand.

"Well, that sucks," he said.

"What was that dear?"

Armitage glanced over at his cohabiting tax partner of thirty years, six months, eighteen days. She sat engrossed in the latest broadcast of *Jessica*'s yogalates exercise regime whilst crocheting a rainbow-coloured scarf that was growing snakelike over her protruding stomach. He moved their stuffed unicorn off the sofa and slumped down into the ageing furniture's overstuffed embrace. "I have a cold," he sighed.

His cohabiting tax partner of thirty years, six months, eighteen days almost dropped a stitch. *Jessica* didn't miss a beat, however. She just slid gracefully into the *unicorn's repose*. Armitage let his eyes follow the instructor's supple curves and toned physique. It would help soothe him from the oncoming barrage.

"You've got a cold?" his cohabiting partner of thirty years, six months, eighteen days screeched, her harsh, piggy eyes almost popping out of their weeping sockets. "Why on the Megabrand's Global Economy did you go and catch one of those?"

Armitage shrugged. "I didn't know I had one," he muttered. "I've not even sneezed."

The podgy fingers of his cohabiting tax partner of thirty years, six months, eighteen days resumed their fidgety twitching movements as the rainbow yarn started to knot once more in its precise, regimented pattern. "Just like you that is. Go out and catch a cold and not even know it. What am I supposed to do now?"

Jessica stretched a long leg up behind her slender neck and formed the *unicorn rampant* pose.

"Perhaps this thing is on the snark?" He tentatively prodded at the back of his hand.

"That's just like you, that is," his cohabiting tax partner of thirty years, six months and eighteen days, grumbled. "Blame everybody else but yourself. That's why you're still a domestic service employee. Bottom of the ladder, unable to make decisions.

"Not like your brother."

Armitage closed his eyes. Here it came.

"No, not like him, at all. He knows where it's at. All that rugby playing got him exactly where he should be — a chartered accountant. If it wasn't for the likes of your brother we would still be in that awful global financial mess. They swept through us like a dose of Multinational Megabrand patent bowel cleanser. They totted up the figures, worked out where the negative capital was and did away with it."

Jessica had taken a break for five minutes and an advert showed scruffy wannabe actors pretending to be homeless in a neatly manicured shopping precinct working together on making socks. "See how life is for the other side in our latest show: *Street Crochet!*" announced the slogan.

"And you know what the first thing they eliminated was, don't you?"

"Sick days."

"And what was the cause of most sick days?"

"The common cold." It was a mantra that Armitage had learnt all the way through his education at the local Multinational Megabrand Mind Academy. Illness was a weakness that threatened every civilisation. It prevented happy workers from undertaking their thrilling, worthwhile jobs and enjoying the great entertainment that Multinational Megabrand provided on every compulsory television in every room of every house that played on loop twenty-four hours a day (the enforced entertainment act had come into power shortly after the cure for the common cold). Once the common cold had been eradicated, there had been no more poverty or sickness. All those who had suffered from it had been cured.

Armitage thought about the cure. He thought about the Multinational Megabrand patient service drone that would arrive shortly and the infernally hot incinerator in its belly that belched fumes as it flew haphazardly through the sky.

He desperately wished that the adverts would end and *Jessica* would come back on. Her yogalates was so relaxing. Not like her previous show: *Tai Kwon Boxing.* That had been linked with a rapid rise in unfortunate groin strains so had been promptly axed after just six excruciating episodes.

Another ad was showing. Five quirky individuals talked secretly about each other's crocheted beanies and made humorous comments as they marked each other's efforts whilst riding home atop a luxury drone.

Armitage looked up at the five ceramic unicorns that frolicked on top of the television, their rainbow manes and tails swishing gaily with free abandon.

"You're just downright selfish," his cohabiting tax partner of thirty years, six months and eighteen days continued. "How will I survive without your pathetic, little income? Do you expect me to go out and work? I guess I should have seen this coming. My mother did warn me.

She told me that I was spending the rest of my financial life with the wrong brother, but did I listen? No, I just ran off into the night on the whim of a young girl who had more romantic notions than... mmph... hummph... mmph!

Her berating words died into struggling gasps of breath as Armitage forced more and more of the rainbow coloured yarn down into her fat mouth. Her piggy eyes bulged as she struggled ineffectively to bat him away with her weak, wobbly arms. Armitage could not help but think that she resembled a unicorn vomiting rainbows. As his tormentor choked her last, *Jessica* gracefully resumed her show and slid into the *acceptant unicorn* pose, but Armitage had no time to watch right now. He had more pressing matters to attend to.

BING BONG!

The Multinational Megabrand patient service drone lacked the two things which would have made its existence that bit more bearable.

Arms.

BING BONG!

So it was that, rather than pressing the button on Armitage's house, it was instead playing the pre-recorded simulation of what it had been programmed to accept as a perfect simulacrum of a domestic doorbell.

BING BONG!

Armitage felt his patented Multinational Megabrand fillings shudder agonisingly in his teeth as he dragged the lifeless corpse of his erstwhile cohabiting tax partner of thirty years, six months and eighteen days to the front door.

She was rather heavy so the task was slow and somewhat laborious. The task was also causing blood to seep through the bandage that he had tied tightly around his hand. It stung like a splintered crochet hook.

BING BONG!

Armitage finally reached the front door and elbowed it opens it with a breathy grunt. The giant behemoth hovered awkwardly before him. One of its rotors was spinning at a slightly slower speed than the others, causing it to list to one side. It was covered in dust and grime from the numerous chimneys that were arranged along its spine like a stylised dorsal fin. The industrial filth covered ripped and faded stickers that publicised other services of Multinational Megabrand and flickering video screens that looped trailers for upcoming crochet reality shows.

Plastered on the front of the semi-sentient automaton was the ubiquitous arse-branded unicorn.

Having nowhere else to really look, Armitage addressed the mythological mascot. "Good afternoon."

"PLEASE PLACE YOUR HAND IN THE SCANNER."

A rusted receptacle attached to a frayed cable tumbled out of the Multinational Megabrand patient service drone and clanked on the surface of the driveway. Armitage cautiously picked it up and slotted the hand of his erstwhile cohabiting tax partner of thirty years, six months and eighteen days inside.

"THERE IS A COVERING OVER THE HAND."

"She cut it this morning," Armitage explained. "Her hand slipped whilst she was crocheting a scarf. They were new hooks. Very sharp."

"ADJUSTING SCANNER TO COMPENSATE."

Armitage held the hand as steadily as he could whilst the Multinational Megabrand patient service drone fizzed, popped and whirred. Its faulty propeller stuttered and it lurched momentarily before righting itself.

"*THERE IS NO PULSE.*"

"It was a very deep cut."

The Multinational Megabrand patient service drone seemed to ponder this to the best of its limited ability before its neural time and motion interface relay decided that it was taking far too long on this particular job and prompted the machine to slide open its human-shaped receptacle.

"*PLACE THE PATIENT IN THE RECEPTA...*" All the lights on the machine died, its rotors stopped spinning and the overworked bucket of bolts crashed to the floor. All the advertising screens flickered and went blue.

Armitage sighed, propped his rapidly stiffening erstwhile cohabiting tax partner of thirty years, six months and eighteen days up against the Multinational Megabrand patient service drone and walked around to the back of the machine where there resided a giant red toggle switch. He flicked the switch off then back on again and returned to the front.

Slowly, the machine growled back into life. The rotors whirred, causing it to limp unsteadily up into the air, cheerful music beeped and booped as the operating system on the screens rebooted before playing more adverts for crochet reality shows and the speaker coughed static.

"*YOU HAVE AIDED THIS MULTINATIONAL MEGABRAND PATIENT SERVICE DRONE BY TERMINATING AND REACTIVATING THE MANUALLY ASSISTED POWER INDUCER. PLEASE RECEIVE THIS FREE GIFT AS A TOKEN OF OUR APPRECIATION.*"

There was a loud popping noise as something dropped out of the belly of the beast.

"THE TERM 'FREE'," continued the Multinational Megabrand patient service drone, *"IS A TERM NOT COVERED BY CURRENT FINANCIAL LAW AND YOU WILL BE CHARGED TWENTY MEGABUCKS FOR THIS GIFT. PLEASE PLACE THE PATIENT IN THE RECEPT-ACLE."*

Armitage grunted and groaned as he manhandled the flabby bulk of his erstwhile cohabiting tax partner of thirty years, six months and eighteen days into the large slot which subsequently slammed back into the Multinational Megabrand patient service drone. There was a large belch of smoke as its internal furnace began its work, then it lurched up into the air, gradually spraying incinerated remains from its chimneys as it did so.

Armitage watched for a moment as the machine lumbered away into the cloudy sky. When it was no more than a hazy smudge, he walked over to the free gift that the automaton had dumped on his driveway, picked it up and dusted it down. It was an entertainment disc entitled *How Yogalates Can Improve The Taste Of Your Coffee.* On the cover was *Jessica* posing in *suggestive unicorn.*

Apparently, the day was getting better.

Armitage smiled and went back inside.

Prodigy

"Well, *obviously* we are so *very* pleased with Charlie's progress."

A perfectly chilled bottle of Chardonnay was tilted and crisply fragranced wine poured into an expensive crystal glass. Harrison smiled and raised the receptacle to his lips before sipping slowly. He had to admit it was a very fine flavour and made the prolonged torture of his hosts' waffling somewhat more bearable. "So what can he do these days?" He volunteered the question in the pretence that he was genuinely interested. In truth, he would much rather have been out on the golf course enjoying the sun on his face and the adoring looks of the rather cute caddy that had recently started carrying his clubs.

"Oh, all sorts of things!" Charlie's mother chipped in brightly.

Harrison groaned inwardly. That was all he needed; the blonde vacuum had been switched on. How Clarke could live with such a ditz was completely beyond him. He may be interminably dull but had an incredibly incisive brain. Perhaps it was just the sex? Anyway, now she had started to witter on, there would be no stopping her. He took a larger sip of the finely fragranced wine and braced himself.

"There's all that clever stuff with the letters, isn't there Ronnie?"

"Algebra, Dear."

"Yes, that's right. Algebra," she giggled, scooping a few pretzels out of a lacquered fair trade bowl from Borneo. "I mean, who would have thought? Sums using letters! What will be next? Stories written in numbers?"

Her childish giggle seared into Harrison's brain like a stun gun into an unlucky future pork chop. He surreptitiously glanced at his watch. Christ! It was only three! He took a mental breath. "Algebra? Really? Fascinating. How old is the little man, now?"

"He's not five until September," Clarke said. "He'll be one of the oldest children in his year group. I guess that will give him a bit of an advantage."

"Five?" Harrison spluttered. "He's not even started school yet and you've got him solving algebraic equations?"

Clarke shook his head. "Oh, the basic stuff he got very quickly. He's onto quadratic formulae and measuring the gradients of tangents now."

The base of Harrison's empty glass rapped against the occasional table as he lowered it down. "Are you serious? Isn't that A-level stuff? For teenagers?"

"Ronnie says it's all a matter of just learning the methods," Charlie's mother beamed. "I think it's all very clever. I struggle to remember the method for making bread rolls."

I bet you'd forget the method to breathe if you were distracted by a Gucci *handbag*: Harrison mused inwardly. Outwardly, he said, "Shouldn't he be more into running around with a cardboard box on his head at his age? I know my two were. They spent six months talking to each other in duck-speak. The constant quacking drove me mad."

"He's never really been into all that infantile stuff," Clarke explained. "He was such a fast learner when it came to reading and was always asking about numbers. That's why we got him the nanny. She's been a great help."

"Oh, she's very good," Charlie's mum exclaimed in a deeply serious manner. "She's from *Hungaria*."

"Bulgaria, dear," Clarke corrected, patiently. "She's from Bulgaria."

Another stun bolt lacerated Harrison's brain as the blonde laughed at her own obvious stupidity. "Silly me! I always get it wrong. But, yes, she is *very* good. So efficient. I suppose they have to be *over there*. What with them being communists and all."

Clarke appeared somewhat uncomfortable as he shifted in his armchair. "Darling," he placed his hand on hers, "we've already had this conversation. They're not communists anymore. They're normal people. Just like you and me."

Heaven help the Hungarians: thought Harrison.

The pen glided fluidly over the paper. Letters danced with numbers and symbols that were completely alien to Hayley Clarke. She accepted that she had never been one of the high flyers at school but she appreciated beauty when she saw it. The fine cut of a *Versace* dress, the high polish of a pair of *Dolce & Gabbana* heels and the mathematical genius of her four-year-old son. Careful, so as not to crease her white, pristine dress, she knelt on the floor next to where Charlie was writing in his exercise book. To a distant onlooker he would look like any other pre-schooler doodling in a drawing book, but in reality...

In reality, what was it that her son was doing?

There were brackets, letters, large numbers, small numbers and all manner of symbols that looked like they belonged on a coat worn by Harry Potter rather than coming from the mind of a child.

Hayley smiled and fussed her son's hair.

He did not even blink. He just carried on writing.

The muffled sound of a foot on thick carpet caught her attention. She turned to face the young woman who had entered the room. "Oh, hello Anna." Hayley motioned to the large tumbler in the nanny's hand. "Is it lunchtime already?"

"Yes, Mrs Clarke. Charlie?"

The young boy looked up immediately.

"Time for your shake."

Quietly and with no protest, the young boy left his work and headed over to the broad, oak dining table where he sat and waited patiently as his nanny placed the tumbler on a coaster. "Drink it all up, now," the young woman instructed.

Charlie did as he was asked, silently gulping the thick drink down until the glass was empty and he was sporting a white moustache that he absentmindedly removed with the back of his hand. Afterwards, he slid off his chair and returned to his work.

"Anna?"

"Yes, Mrs Clarke?"

"Can I ask what is *actually* in the shakes you give, Charlie?"

"Good things," the nanny replied as she carried the

empty tumbler through to the kitchen. "Things to make him learn well."

"Darling?"

Ronald Clarke mumbled a vague response from his side of the bed.

"Do you think Charlie is happy?"

The grey-haired professor turned wearily onto his back. It had been a long day. Too many meetings and *other* things... He flinched at the memory and his hand absentmindedly rubbed his cheek. "Why shouldn't he be?"

"I don't know. It's just that when Mark came over the other day, I got the feeling he didn't *approve*, you know?"

Clarke sighed. "I can't say that I do."

His wife continued on with her train of thought, regardless: "And he's so quiet."

"Who? Mark Harrison?"

"No. *Charlie*. All he does is write out those sums in his book. All day long. I know it's all very clever and that, but is it normal?"

"Well, we know he's not normal by society's standards. He's a genius. We should be proud of that." Clarke turned back towards his soft pillow. It truly had been a long day. He wanted to go to sleep and forget all about it.

His wife apparently had other ideas.

"And then there's that *stuff* that Anna feeds him."

"You mean the shakes?" Clarke groaned into his pillow. "We've been over this before, Darling."

"Yes, yes, I know," Hayley flapped. "They're full of omega things to help his brain do what it needs to do. I know all that, but surely it wouldn't help to give him something else for a change?"

"Such as?"

"Oh, I don't know..." She tapped a manicured finger against her perfect lips. "Something *fun*. Something like a jam sandwich, perhaps?"

"So you want to fill him full of junk?"

"No..."

"Right then."

"But, those shakes... What's in them?"

"I told you..."

"Yes, I know. But *what* ingredients, exactly?"

Ronald Clarke realised that he did not really know.

"I told you, Mister Clarke, things to help him learn."

"Yes, I know that, Anna, but *what* exactly?"

The dark-haired nanny eyed her employer suspiciously. "You've never cared before. Why do you want to know now?"

"It's..." Clarke squirmed, "my wife that wants to know."

The nanny raised an eyebrow. "Oh, so today you care about what *she* thinks, do you?" Acid dripped from her tongue. "Yesterday it was 'She means nothing to me,' and 'Marrying her was a mistake.' I think you need to decide what it is that you want from your life." She crossed her arms accusingly across her small bust.

Clarke flinched as he expected another slap, but none came. This was too much to endure. "This obviously isn't working," he muttered. "I think we will have to terminate your employment. I will pay you a month's wages but you have to be out of the house by the weekend."

He turned and scurried out of the room, his lover's eyes burning hatred into his back.

Hayley sipped from the hot cappuccino as she watched Charlie at the table. Gone were the maths books. Gone were the long numbers and funny-looking symbols. Instead, he had a large colouring book out in front of him and he was doodling with a pack of pencil crayons. From her spot on the sofa, it looked like he was drawing a man of some sort. It was bright red with its arms out to its sides. Perhaps it was a cartoon character, a superhero of some type? That would explain the bright, vibrant scarlet.

Whatever it was, it was better than algebra.

Anna walked quietly into the room. "Mrs. Clarke."

The mother nodded at the nanny. In her hand, the brunette was holding a tumbler that was full to the brim with a bright red shake. Well, at least it *looked* unhealthy; that was a start, at least. Besides, the woman would be gone from their house in a few days and Hayley could start being a proper mother again, spoiling and pampering her little man.

She looked on as Anna gave the drink to Charlie and he glugged it down voraciously. "Wow, that must be really tasty. What's in it?"

The nanny removed the empty tumbler and gently ran her fingers through the young boy's hair. "Something to make him happy," she said. "Something to make him happy."

Hayley woke with a start. She had been dreaming. It had been such a *sweet* dream too. Ronnie and she had been walking along a deserted beach with Charlie. The three of them had been hand-in-hand and smiling contentedly. She had been wearing a long, white flowing dress and her feet had felt warm in the sand. The sea had been shushing against the shore and dolphins had been diving in and out of the surf.

An idyllic paradise.

Then there had been lightning and thunder. A massive clap had shot out through the air and she had woken in a panic.

Her heart pounded as she sat bolt upright in bed, her eyes wide open and her hair plastered to her scalp.

The light was on.

Why was the light on?

Ronnie was stirring next to her as she turned and saw that they were not alone. Charlie was standing at the foot of the bed in his nightwear.

"Sweetie?" she asked. "What's the matter?"

Her son stood silent in his brown, checked pyjamas his eyes off in some middle distance.

"He's sleepwalking," Ronald grumbled, slipping his glasses on and peering over the tops of them as he always did. "God knows why."

Hayley slipped out of the bed and went over to her son. Gently, she slipped her arm around his shoulders. "Come on, sweetie. Let's get you back to bed." Silently, Charlie did as he was told and followed his mother back to his bedroom. Hayley gave a small gasp when she opened the door. There were drawings everywhere. Reams and reams of sketches and doodles. All of them were pictures of people or parts of people in vibrant red crayon. She stooped down and picked one up then wished that she had not. It was the inside of someone's head: the muscle, tissue and fibre.

"Oh, Charlie!" she cried. "No wonder you were having nightmares." Carefully she led him to his bed, lifted him up and tucked him in. When she was sure that he was soundly asleep she scooped up all the sketches and marched back to her bedroom.

"Ronnie! Have you seen these?" Hayley demanded, thrusting the pictures under her husband's nose. "What the hell is going on?"

Clarke leafed through the images and shrugged. "So he has a thing about anatomy? What's the problem?"

All Hayley could do was stare at her husband, dumbfounded.

"At least it's not maths," Clarke grumbled and, dropping the pictures to the floor, settled back down to sleep.

Hayley lay awake listening to every noise in the house. There was the scratching of the tree against the window, the creaking of their bed as her husband shifted in his sleep, the ticking of the bedside clock. The list was endless. It was an unwelcome symphony of music being played with extreme vigour by an unseen orchestra intent on keeping her from her sleep.

She tried burying her head in her pillow.

She tried going to sleep with her arms crossed over her ears.

Nothing worked so she just lay there and listened. Listened to the scratch, the creak, the tick.

Scratch, creak, tick,

Scratch, creak, tick,

Scratch, creak, *thud*, tick.

Hayley held her breath and listened again. There had been another noise, a rogue instrument in the nocturnal orchestration. She peered over at Ronald. He was sound asleep and she was sure that he would be none too pleased if she woke him again.

With as much stealth as she could manage, she swung her legs out of the warm bed and made her way to the door. Cautiously, she peered down the landing.

Nothing moved in the shadows.

There came another *thud.* It was downstairs.

Hayley glanced back nervously into the bedroom. She could wake Ronald. She could ring the police. She could do any number of things but she would be overreacting. Instead, she cautiously made her way along the dark landing. Her hand hovered momentarily over the light switch then drew back. What if it was an intruder? A light would draw them to her.

She edged down the stairs in darkness.

At first, everything seemed as she had left it when she had gone up to bed. The front door was closed and the curtains were drawn. Nothing out of the norm.

The living room door, however, was open.

Had she shut it?

Perhaps she had left it open?

Hayley could not remember.

She crept away from the bottom stair and padded over to the door in her bare feet, her short nightie brushing against her thighs. Suddenly she felt cold and exposed. A shiver ran down her spine.

As she carefully made her way into the living room, she became aware of the notion that she was not alone. There was a light noise from behind the sofa. Her heart rising up in her throat, she crept as stealthily as she could towards the sofa, the thick pile of the carpet pressing up between her bare toes. The woman held her breath tighter than she had ever held her handbag on a crowded bus and her heart felt like it was going to pound out of her chest. Every instinct was telling her to turn and flee but she had to know what was down here, what was hiding.

Slowly, tentatively, the thick pile masking the sound of her hesitant footsteps, Hayley ventured around to the rear of the sofa, her eyes starting to become accustomed to the gloom and the varying depths of the shadows. The tension she felt knotting up inside her was unbearable; it was as if she had been trussed up in an over-tight corset, unable to free herself.

One hand steadying herself on the top of the sofa, she peered around its back.

There was nothing there.

Absolutely nothing.

Hayley let out an immense groan and breathed in sweet relief as she sank back against the finely up-holstered piece of furniture. It was okay. Everything was okay. It had just been her imagination.

She shrieked in pain as something sharp dug into her ankle.

Looking down she saw a knife sticking out from under the sofa, clutched in a small hand.

Hayley turned to run but her foot would not move properly. As she twisted and fell she could only watch in disbelief as her small son crawled out from between the legs of the sofa.

Anna flicked on the lights and let a feeling of satisfaction draw a smile to her lips. Charlie was sat slumped over a stack of drawings that lay strewn around the dining table. The nanny tiptoed over and slowly stroked his hair as she carefully leafed through the perfectly articulated sketches of human anatomy. Her finger traced the ventricles of a heart, the workings of a lower intestine and the musculature of dissected torsos – male and female.

She nodded with approval. He had been most meticulous; there was not a drop of blood on any of the drawings.

The same could not be said for the rest of the house.

Carefully, lovingly, she scooped the young genius up in her arms and carried him out to her waiting car.

Matilda

It was hot. Unbearably hot.

Matilda lay sprawled out on the lawn chair in her neatly trimmed back garden. The sun blazed down and she closed her eyes against its searing rays. There was shade elsewhere in the garden, some trees provided a modicum of dappled shade over by the willow fence, but she could not be bothered to move. It required just too much effort.

She was getting old.

She knew that now and, more importantly, she accepted it. Not graciously, not at all. No, she despised the fact that her once sleek, youthful body was now no longer capable of the things that it used to be. No, she just lay out in the scorching summer sun, closed her eyes and glowered at all who came near her.

Matilda just wanted to be left alone. She had no idea how much longer she had left but she knew instinctively that the number of days in front of her was far, far less than those behind her and she just wanted to be left in peace for the dwindling amount of time that she had left.

From time to time, visitors dropped by either for a perfunctory visit or just to be generally nosey, so she either turned her back on them and ignored them or made her feelings quite clearly known, depending on how her mood took her at that particular moment.

This was not how old age was supposed to be, surely? She had never really known her parents. Her father had never been on the scene and she had been separated from her mother when she was still very young. She never knew why. One of life's mysteries, like why did you have to pee so much more when you were in your twilight years? When she was younger she could go for hours, now though…

Matilda let out a sigh. If her erstwhile lovers could see her now: frail, feeble and incontinent. Not like when she had been younger. She had had her pick of the bunch. She would wander around town, her head held high and take her pick of all the attractive males that tickled her fancy. Whoever, whenever, wherever: there had been no limits to her passions.

No children though. Funny that. Not once had there been a little slip or an accident. Perhaps she just had not remained with anyone long enough to try for a family? Whatever the reason, perhaps it had been for the best? What sort of a mother would she have made? Imagine being knee-deep in wailing, mewling offspring? The acrid scent of them constantly pissing themselves and the sickening noise of their constant petulance.

No, she would not have made a good mother. Not at all. Matilda smiled to herself. Thank heaven for small mercies.

Her eyes snapped open, her reverie disrupted.

She was not alone.

The birds in the trees that had been twittering so loudly had fallen incriminatingly silent. Something had spooked them.

Matilda growled under her breath as she scanned the garden with her failing eyesight. These days, anything as far as the willow fence was just a blur. Her sense of smell, though, was as sharp as ever and she took a deep breath.

The scent that hit her was unmistakable.

It was a young stud that she had known some months previous. They had undertaken a quick, torrid affair before he had disappeared and never returned. It seemed that he was back and most likely wanting to rekindle their fire.

Matilda's fire, however, had been doused by the waters of old age. Perhaps that was why she urinated more these days?

The young male sauntered into the garden as if he owned the place. Some years ago, Matilda would have not let him dare. She would have challenged such audacity and chased him out with his tail between his legs. Now, though, she could not be bothered. She just rolled over on the lawn chair and presented the youngster with her uninterested back.

She felt a prod on her spine. He was not for taking a hint.

Matilda sighed her disinterest.

There was another prod.

Matilda turned her head to glower at the young upstart.

At least, she tried to

Pressure on her cheek pushed her face down into the cushions of the lawn chair and she felt a heavy weight mounting up onto her back.

This could not be happening!

Frantically, she urged all the effort she had stored in her aching limbs to roll out from under the mass of her unwanted paramour. She slid and snaked off the side of the chair onto the warm, freshly mown grass. Landing on her feet she stared at the intruder, venom in her eyes. He sat upright on the chair, looking for all the world like it belonged to him. For a short while they just remained that way, staring at each other: he young and cocksure; her, older and not wanting to enter into a fight.

Years ago, she would have lain the law down immediately. She would have swiped him across the face and left him bloodied for his audacity. Now though…

Now Matilda felt something inside her that had never raised its ugly head before. Fear. Her stomach was tense and her mouth was dry. She knew that he was far stronger than her and exceptionally agile. He could take her. He could pin her down. He could…

He could try.

She was not sure where it came from, but in an instant, Matilda was lunging up at the youth. For a split second, she inhabited the body of someone far, far younger. Her legs pushed her up and her mouth opened in a war cry as she catapulted herself at the wide-eyed assailant. He cried out in shock as she hammered into his chest and barrelled him off the other side of the lawn chair.

They hit the ground with an almost silent impact. Matilda felt a sense of joy wash over her. The satisfaction that she had managed to pull off such a manoeuvre at her age filled her with pride. However, it was a pride that was short-lived when she went to pull herself up and one of her legs gave way to a sharp spasm.

She cursed her age-wracked body as the youth rolled away and propelled himself forward once more. Matilda desperately tried to crawl away but something sharp slashed across her back and she screamed as she knew that she had been cut.

She also knew that she could not win.

She had to retreat. Quickly.

Clawing at the hard, sun-baked ground, Matilda frantically dragged herself out from under her attacker. She felt another sharp blow across her rear as she managed to scramble to her shaking feet and put as much effort as she could into bolting out of the garden which, if she were not successful, would become the place of her untimely demise.

She paid no attention as to where she was running. She just fled forwards, her legs working by the memory of running alone. She had no strength left, just sheer determination to survive another day. Just one more day, a peaceful one, so that she could curl up and die in peace, not at the hands of a young, brutish rapist.

She looked neither left nor right as she staggered out of the driveway down the side of the house. She was too fixed on ensuring that her legs did not give way beneath her. She did not see the family saloon as it cruised down the quiet, suburban road. She was only vaguely aware of the screech of brakes then there was the excruciating sensation that everything in her body was somehow displaced.

The world spun around her. The floor momentarily became the sky until it rushed up to greet her in a painful, treacherous embrace.

Then there was stillness. She lay on the hot tarmac, her life ebbing away and she was aware of the sound of her front door opening and slamming shut, followed by frantic footsteps of someone running down the driveway towards her.

Then she was flying, scooped up into the arms of an angel. Water splashed her face and she tried in vain to lick it, thinking it would quench the burning agony.

And then there was nothing.

Nothing but a distraught woman cradling the limp body of her dead cat.

Test Flight

Goldblum grappled with the joystick as the plane jinked and jerked from side to side. The webbing dug in tight whilst his eyes widened at the sight of the cliff face looming rapidly like a ravening giant.

At the last moment, his hands flew from the controls to instinctively cover his face from the inevitable collision.

Saunders tutted sympathetically as his associate pulled yet another lifeless body out of the X-20 simulator. Feeling the lack of pulse on the latest test pilot, he turned and asked of his fellow technician, "Do you think we've made this thing rather too realistic?"

Scratchcard Man

It was a fresh summer's evening and the dried, worn grass crunched under Scratchcard Man's sensible footwear as he made his way over to the red-brick modern housing estate. He smiled to himself as he inhaled the fragrant aroma of roses and lavender that lazily sauntered up from the municipal flower bed and he chuckled whilst bending to fuss the fluffy grey tomcat that had been following him.

Yes, he had a good feeling about tonight. The weather was clement and windows were open to allow the fragrant summer air unhindered access to the small modern-builds that filled this particular estate. People would be relaxed and in a more welcoming mood than if it had been lashing down with rain or blustery with a gale. When the weather was rough they just battened down the hatches and ignored his friendly rat-a-tat as he walked his rounds purveying the little scratchcards that could liberate them from their mundane lives with promises of an instantaneous win of ten thousand pounds, tax-free.

Scratchcard Man beamed at the idea of their delighted faces after scratching off a winning number. There would be the hesitation as they wondered whether it was in fact correct, then their mouth would start to edge up into a tentative smile and they would get that little excited tremble in their shoulders before they glanced up at him with such a look of wonder and joy. They would thank him in such a profuse manner that he would bashfully have to say he was just doing his job and that they now needed to contact the promoters whose web address could be found on the back of the scratchcard before he waved a cheery goodbye and happily carried on to the next address on his list.

That was how he imagined it. As of yet there had been no winners.

But there was time.

There must be one somewhere. Perhaps in this estate? It was new to him. It was on the neatly typed list that he had received just that morning from the promoters. He didn't know what they promoted. He didn't really care. All he knew was that they sent him the scratchcards and the lists of houses that he had to visit. The rest was up to him.

Spread a little happiness in this corner of an otherwise dull, bleak earth.

And what happiness he spread, indeed. As he walked from house to house children would follow him as if he were some modern Pied Piper. "The Scratchcard Man! The Scratchcard Man!" they would sing as he travelled along the jostling streets and narrow allies. The smiles of the young always brought him so much joy. Their innocence hadn't yet been sullied by the corruption and wickedness that polluted the world these days. He knew that to be the case because it had been said so on breakfast television and in the newspapers. Scratchcard Man allowed himself a little frown at that thought but rapidly pushed the grey cloud of gloom away as he rounded a corner to the first row of houses on his list.

This was a new customer.

New customers always bought well. He guessed it was because they were just so glad to have someone reach out to them and offer them a way out of their hum-drum, downtrodden lives. He could not begin to imagine what it must be like for the poor souls: one of the couple out all day working a thankless task for a pittance of pay whilst the other was trapped at home with housework, confined by four small walls whilst the smartly-dressed people of daytime television smiled at how wonderful it was that they were moving to a much larger, swankier house in the country. Scratchcard Man could only think that it must induce such debilitating despair. Imagine the doldrums it would cast the poor couple down into? There would be tears. There would be rows. Heaven forbid, there could even be divorce.

Scratchcard Man shook his head sadly then drew a deep breath, smiled his bestest, smiliest smile and knocked brightly on the faded wooden door that was in desperate need of a new coat of paint. He was here to change their life for the better.

He waited patiently as he listened to the approach-ing footsteps and the rattling of the door handle. His best-est, smiliest smile was fit to burst with pride from his face when the door swung inwards and a petite, young woman peered around its protective shield. "Hello?" she inquired. "Can I help you?"

"Scratchcard Man!" beamed Scratchcard Man.

The young woman looked perplexed. She pushed a stray dark hair back behind her ear. "I'm sorry? I don't..."

"You're new. You're on my list." He pulled his neatly

typed list out from his inside pocket and presented it to her with overwhelming glee.

She frowned as her eyes wandered over the blank piece of tatty A4 paper. Nervously, she backed inside and made to shut the door.

Scratchcard Man would not be deterred from his mission of charity. This poor woman needed saving from her mundane lifestyle. "New buyers always buy well," he explained seriously as he wedged his sensible shoe against the bottom of the door.

The woman became frantic. She shoved hard against the door trying to dislodge the intruder's foot. However, she was slight and he was much taller and did not budge.

"New buyers always buy well," Scratchcard Man tutted as he waved the brightly coloured scratchcards in front of her. "You can win up to ten thousand pounds, tax free. There is a web address on the back for the promoters."

The woman stared in disbelief at the neatly trimmed pieces of cereal box that the madman was waggling maniacally in front of her. She drew back her arm and made to slap him or push him away but the crazy guy was too quick and he grabbed her hand as it swung towards him.

"Your mundane existence is just unacceptable," Scratchcard Man sighed as he tucked his little cardboard tickets to freedom away. "I have come to liberate you." With that, he reached inside his jacket and there was a vicious flash of steel in the evening sun.

The woman sank back into the doorway. Her stomach felt wet and everything was going grey...

Scratchcard Man tidied up and quietly closed the

door behind him so as not to disturb the poor woman. She must have been very sleepy to nod off like that. He replaced the knife in his inside pocket and drew out the list as he walked away from the house. He smiled with glee as he saw there was another new customer just down the road.

New customers always bought well.

Another mundane life to liberate.

He had been right; this was going to be a very good evening indeed.

Biscuit Tin Of Doom

Trevor Peavey looked at the biscuit tin.

The biscuit tin looked at Trevor Peavey.

Its glossy metal lid proclaimed that there were wonders and delights stored within: ginger biscuits, chocolate fingers, sugar sprinkled shortbread and other such delicacies to tantalise the tastebuds. Trevor Peavey knew otherwise.

One of the girls from *Klassy Kouture* had dropped by this morning with a waft of overpowering scent and a red, glossy smile. She had presented the tin as a gift to the staff of *One Stop Wardrobe*, wished them well and minced her high-heeled way back down the high street to her tacky little boutique.

Beware of Greeks bearing gifts, thought the overweight, balding store manager as he rubbed his sweaty palms against the grey, pinstripe material of his practical, utilitarian suit. What were they playing at? Never had those young harpies ever shown any friendship or goodwill towards him and his staff. What was this really about?

He had his theories. Oh, yes he did.

Witches.

That's what the scantily clad girls down the road were. They enticed the customers in with their charms and spells then, when they had the poor souls mesmerised, they magicked their plastic out of their wallets before sending them packing laden down with flashy bags of cheap Indian imports. Why else would anyone purchase any of their tacky items of tat?

And now they were trying to take out the competition.

Beware of Greeks bearing gifts. This was a Trojan Horse if ever he had seen one. It had to be, but what little surprise did it hide within?

It was not biscuits, that was for sure.

In his mind's eye, Peavey saw himself prying open the lid only to be sucked down into a maelstrom-like portal to some sort of fiery hell dimension. First, his head would be stretched out towards the swirling cataclysm that spun like an angry tornado. He would scream in agony as every millimetre of skin and tissue was sucked and warped towards the ravenous mouth. To no avail, his hand would try desperately to cling onto the melamine surface of the staff room table and there would be a terrible squelching noise as his body was passed through the metaphysical wringer depositing him alone and unaided in a world where screams and shrieks of agony carried on the wind that stank of sulphur.

Or perhaps when he opened the lid there would be tentacles, long green tentacles? They would lurch out of the tin in one fluid movement and wrap their powerful suckers around his helpless form. Their titanic grip would pin his arms immobile to his side and he would not even be able to reach for his trusty Swiss Army knife that he always carried in his pocket. Trevor Peavy would feel his feet spring from the tiled floor as he was vaulted up over the tin by the swaying mass and he would peer down into their midst, wailing in horror as a vicious beak snapped open and shut beneath him. He would wriggle frantically trying to escape but the grasp of the creature would constrict tighter around him as all he could hope for would be the bliss of unconsciousness when it pulled him down to be devoured piece by piece.

But what if it was a banshee? Imagine that! He would open up the lid expecting to find some sweet, biscuity morsel only to observe an ethereal green smoke waft out into the staff room. He would stand transfixed as it drifted lazily around the sink and then through the handle of the rather nice mug which he had saved the vouchers for from those packets of tea bags that time. Then it would curl seductively between the table legs before winding its way around him in a *come hither my dear* manner before coalescing into the form of a beautiful young woman with cascading blonde hair and the sweetest blue eyes. Peavey, the lifelong bachelor, would feel relief wash over him at the thought that this was not too bad after all only to then cringe in terror as the phantasm opened her mouth and the noise began to emanate from her stretching lips. A noise like the moan of a thousand mothers grieving the deaths of a thousand children would begin to echo around the room and assault his eardrums. He would drop to his knees, his hands vainly covering his ears whilst the banshee's mouth grew wider and wider, contorting her beautiful face into an obscene monstrosity. All the while the screech would increase in volume and intensity until, finally, Peavey's head would explode with a sickening *pop*, splattering his brains across the staff notice board.

It could even be something worse. What if he opened the box and found it completely empty? He would stand there puzzled and bemused as he felt inside the empty metal tin, as he held it upside down and battered on the base to see if anything came out. Then things would start to happen around the world. There would be earthquakes and famine, plague and drought, war and financial collapse. Experts would be called in by the United Nations to study just what had caused these catastrophes and they would trace them all back to poor Trevor Peavey who had inadvertently opened a Pandora's Box and released countless woes and tribulations on the unsuspecting world. He would be hated and vilified. His life would become null and worthless overnight. His remaining days would be spent being chased from one town to another and no one anywhere would dare to shelter this abhorrent little man until finally, one day, he would drop exhausted on a hillside and carrion birds would descend upon him, pecking his wretched, withered body to death.

No, the tin must never be opened. Whatever it contained would be a vile and devastating creation of wily magicks. It would have to be destroyed.

The staff room door swung open and Gemma from the shoe concession walked in. "Ooo, biccies!" she squealed in delight before opening the tin, choosing a couple of tasty-looking Hob Nobs and making herself a cup of tea.

My Divergent Land

It's cold here.

I cast my eyes out through the fractured panes of stained glass across the barren landscape which has been fashioned by my own actions and I see rain falling on scorched earth. Not the warm, refreshing rain of spring that feeds and nourishes infant plants as they erupt from the warmth of their womb-like soil. No, not that. I watch as the cold, frigid rain of autumn relentlessly batters down all remaining life and foliage, forging it into a pulverised mess of decomposing matter and severed limbs.

These latter are the work of my children.

I close my eyes and listen as their viscous bodies shamble around my sanctuary in a lurching manner. They are my blunt instruments with which I fashioned this world to my liking. Before they rose from the ground, dragging with them the hatred of a cursed and abused planet, society was meaningless and frivolous. People would think nothing of spending a week's wages on a meal for two in a restaurant where the height of cuisine was a strawberry cut into thin slices served upon a smear of melted chocolate.

There are no such places now.

They have all gone, along with their pretentious cli-entele.

There is no place for them in my world, my divergent land.

You see, I grasped reality by the scruff of its flea-ridden pelt and shook it so hard that the blood-sucking parasites were eradicated and the future was changed. It had not been deserving of that which lay waiting for it – a time of peace and harmony. No, it had to be punished for what it had allowed to occur, for the decadence that had seeped insidiously through its veins like a powerful opiate in the bloodstream of a filthy, dirty, self-soiled addict. So I took it and smeared it across my very own fine china plate before carving up its occupants into delicate slivers, fine morsels and arranging them decoratively for my con-sumption.

I made a thing of beauty that no one before had been imbued with the talent to achieve.

But now, this perfect creation of mine is in danger. Forces dare to rise against me. They battle my children and are emboldened by minor victories against my ser-vants. They are led by an old adversary, one whose path crossed mine before I set foot on this, my blessed land.

He, however, cannot harm me and he knows it. He is not a man of virtue; for so it was said, "He who rose like a dragon of old shall be slain by the man of virtue."

No, he is a vile creature with a heart as dark as mine. He will rally his little band of warriors and send them to their deaths, laughing merrily as I wrench their final, gasping breaths from their bleeding, scabrous lungs. No one can touch me, not while I have my playthings in my possession, those items that saw the beginning of creation and remain forever eternal.

I am safe.

I am immortal.

I am Kanor.

Dog Days

Dear Diary.

Well, it's been a rather stressful day, I must say. I had been out in the garden this afternoon tidying up the beans (those Wimple kids from next door had kicked their ball over again) when I came in to find Ethel all a fluster.

"What's the matter?" I ask.

"Oh, Ray," says she, all tearful, "that horrid man has let his wretched dog foul outside our house again."

I sigh to myself. Ethel does get upset by this. I keep telling her it's nothing really, but she won't have it. She won't have it at all.

"I'll just get a bag and clear it up, love," I say but she's flapping around the living room like a mother hen that's lost its chicks.

"But he'll just be back tomorrow!" she wails, her hands yanking at that pink pinny I bought her last year. "He'll just do it again!"

So I sit her down, put the kettle on then go outside and sort what needs sorting. After a nice, warm brew she seemed to settle a bit, but I could tell, come bedtime, that she was still out of sorts. She's gone up to bed and hardly touched her cocoa.

Dear Diary.

Oh dear, it's gotten worse. That business with the dog I mean. I was just walking down the garden path from my potting shed after fixing a pane of glass that the Wimple kids had put through (I really wish their parents would keep them on a tighter leash) when I heard Ethel shouting. I raced down the side of the house and out to the front where there she was, waving her hands in the air and shrieking wildly at that chap with the dog. It's one of those squat little affairs: bandy legs, squashed face, beady eyes. The dog, I mean, not the owner.

It would appear that the dog had once again done its business on the grass verge in front of our house and Ethel had seen red. I won't write down what she said as I'm sure she'd be mightily embarrassed to think that I heard her talking in such a manner, but the man was giving as good as he got. He was effing and blinding, calling her a "Crazy old bat," and other such insults whilst trying to drag his dog away which was desperately trying to make friends with Ethel.

Anyway, I managed to half guide, half drag her back into the house whilst the fellow stormed off down the road, muttering expletives under his breath. Ethel marched into the kitchen and started slamming pots and pans around.

I decided it was safest to leave her to it.

Dear Diary.

Feeling a bit perplexed today. Ethel seems a lot brighter than she has of recent. She went out this morning and when she came back she was positively beaming. I asked her what had put the smile on her face and she said that she had been on the Internet at the local library. They have computers there. Apparently, you can read things from all around the world. She said she had found a *site* (I think that's the right word) that had a solution for the dog mess problem.

I smiled and told her that was brilliant. I then asked her if we were having chicken for dinner as she had one in her shopping bag. She gave me a strange little smile and headed off into the kitchen.

About an hour later, the smell of cooking drew me in after her and I saw her busying herself away at the stove. However, peering over her shoulder gave me a bit of a start. Rather than all the tasty bits of the bird cooking in a stew, there was a pan of thick, red liquid in which bobbed the bird's head and feet.

"Ethel..."

"It's blood, dear. Pig's blood."

"It doesn't look very appetising," I ventured.

"It's not for you, silly."

And it wasn't. We had pork pies for tea. They were very tasty too, but I can't help but wonder what happened to the other stuff. Perhaps she was experimenting at making black pudding.

Dear Diary.

I think something is going on with Ethel but I'm not sure what.

I was on my way back from B&Q with some bamboo canes (the Wimple children had actually climbed into our garden to get their ball back and knocked my runners over – most annoying) when I noticed the strangest thing. The patch of grass where that chap lets his dog defecate had been disturbed. I poked at it with my shoe and it bounced under my toe. I looked up and saw Ethel at the living room window watching and smiling.

After I had taken the canes around the back I went inside to ask her if everything was alright then I noticed that the chap was outside letting his dog do its business again. I steeled myself for another tirade like the other day, but it never came.

Smiling, Ethel turned away from the window. "Everything is fine, Ray," she beamed. "Would you like a cup of tea?"

I'm sure that even now after fifty-three years of marriage I still do not fully understand the female mind.

Dear Diary.

A terrible thing has happened! The chap with the dog has been found dead! Apparently, he lived a couple of streets down from us in one of those new-builds on Harrington Crescent. I visited the corner shop to pick up the paper and his neighbour was there chatting to the girl behind the counter. Something had mauled him to death and eaten his brains. Can you imagine? What an awful way to go. Also, his dog was missing.

Well, I went straight home to tell Ethel. She was just coming in from the garden whistling to herself. "Oh dear," she said with what seemed like a curiously forced nonchalance. "Steak and kidney pie for tea?"

Dear Diary.

Today has been one of those days that I could never have conceived. It all started with those wretched Wimple kids going too far! They actually climbed over the wall into our garden and started pulling out my onions! I saw them from the kitchen and chased them off as they clambered back over the wall. One of the little brats actually had the nerve to stick two fingers up at me. In my day that was just unheard of. I don't know what the world's coming to.

I went straight round and had it out with their father. Well, at least I *tried* to. He's not the sort that really rises to anger, you know? He has long hair and a beard and I think he works at the university. Anyway, he said that he'd have a quiet word with them and was sure that they didn't really mean to cause any harm before wishing me, "Good day," and quietly shutting the door in my face. Stupid man! If I had been caught vandalising someone's property, my father would have put me across his knee. He most certainly would not have sat down and gone all bleeding heart about it.

I stomped back home in quite the rage and was just marching up to my potting shed when Ethel came dashing up behind me all in a flap shouting my name.

"What?" I snapped back. I was in no mood to be bothered right then. I had onions to salvage.

"Come inside, love," she gasped having hurtled up the garden path after me like a steaming locomotive. "I've just put the kettle on. Come and have a brew. It'll calm you down."

I shook my head. "No, dear. I need to get this sorted." I made to open the shed door but Ethel inserted herself in front of me, blocking my way.

"Please, Ray. Later," she begged me, her eyes flickering nervously over her shoulder. "Come and have that cuppa. I've got some Hob Nobs," she grinned nervously as she tried to take hold of my hand.

I yanked myself away and folded my arms across

my chest. "Ethel," I demanded, "what is this about? Are you hiding something?"

She wrung her hands together in her pinny and tears started to run down her cheeks. "Oh, Ray. Oh, Ray. You mustn't go in there."

"Why ever not?"

Then I stopped. I sniffed. I started. Something smelled awful.

I shot Ethel a glance, pushed past and yanked open the door to the shed and there it was, the dog that used to defecate outside our house. Only, it wasn't quite the same. It was strangely different.

"I didn't know what to do, Ray," Ethel was wailing as I lowered myself down onto my haunches to inspect our canine guest. "He came back here afterwards. It must be because he was created here."

I frowned, only half taking in her incessant babbling. What lay in front of me with its muzzle draped over its paw was definitely dog-shaped, but unlike anything else I had ever seen before. Its fur was thinning and its skin was drooping down off its muscles. Its eyes were a pale blue and totally unfocused, not the sort of dark, alert orbs you would expect from a breed like this. Then there was its breath. My God! I know dogs don't have great oral hygiene but this one smelt like it had been drinking out of a cesspit. I covered my mouth with the back of my hand and coughed before asking, "What do you mean by *afterwards* and *created here?*" In truth though a sinking sensation in my stomach was already starting to fill in the gaps.

So, as I crouched there, studying this weirdest of creatures, Ethel explained that she had somewhat lost the plot over all the dog business and had taken it upon herself to exact a certain amount of justice. She had gone to the library and looked up a way to stop the dog from using our grass verge as a toilet and she had inadvertently come across an article about a type of creature that did not need to relieve itself as whatever it ate magically absorbed into its body and sustained it.

She had come home with a ritual to change a living thing into one of these creatures and buried a token where she knew the dog would pass.

That night the transformation had happened and the dog had turned into what now lay snoozing in my shed.

A zombie.

Unfortunately, my darling wife had not really considered the consequences that zombies are somewhat ravenous. Its first act after metamorphosis had been to turn on the nearest living creature: its owner. After that, it had apparently come back looking for its maker and had refused to leave so she had shut it in my potting shed until she could decide what to do with it.

The zombie dog lazily opened one of those misty, far away eyes and regarded me. Its short tail thumped once on the dusty floor. Without giving it a single thought I automatically reached over and tickled it behind the ear. The tail wagged again and it grunted in obvious pleasure.

I stood up, placed my hands on my hips and looked down at our undead guest. "Well I can't say that he *seems* very dangerous," I said.

"He won't be, not to us," Ethel explained, kneeling down and softly stroking the dog on its neck. It rolled over onto its back for more fussing, flaccid skin rolling down its sides and pooling on the floor. "It would appear that zombies are extremely loyal to their creators. They will do whatever we wish and defend us to the end. That could be why he killed his previous owner, because he knew I felt threatened by him. We can't just get rid of him, can we?"

I turned and looked out over my decimated onion bed as a smile formed on my lips. "No, we can't," I agreed, "I think he'll just have to stay."

Smoking Is Bad For Your Health

Abigail Smart looked at the time on her eco-friendly, self-winding wristwatch with a mixture of agitation and annoyance. "This really is quite preposterous," the middle-aged woman grumbled to her partner, Jeremy Whittaker, who was standing next to her, rocking back and forth in his cruelty-free walking boots. "All I want is a small packet of Golden Virginia and they can't manage to get the kiosk open on time."

Whittaker ran his smooth, office desk fingers through his bushy yet immaculately groomed protest beard. "Well, it is Sunday, Darling. Perhaps, they're not quite up to speed yet."

"Up to speed? Up to speed?" Smart shook her head so violently that her fair-trade Guatemalan earrings bounced angrily from side to side. "The wretched supermarket's been open an hour *for browsing*, for pity's sake. They're obviously trying to squeeze as much life out of their underpaid workforce as possible. That's the real reason."

She was about to launch into a pre-prepared lecture on modern slave labour when a young, brown-haired woman briskly approached the kiosk and let herself in behind the counter. The shop assistant was about to apologise for her tardiness when there was a commotion nearby. All eyes in the lengthening line of customers for the cigarette kiosk turned to watch an elderly woman in a dilapidated electric wheelchair skid her creaking vehicle into the front of the queue. She reached into a flapping handbag and slapped a screwed up ten pound note onto the counter.

"Weneee ee anayyy."

The young shop assistant's mouth mimicked the disabled woman's handbag as, in confusion, it too flapped open.

"Weneee ee anayyy," the elderly woman insisted, spittle dribbling down her chin.

"I don't believe it!" Smart hissed under her breath to her partner. To the woman who had pushed in front of her, she said, "Excuse me, but we were first."

The old woman's rheumy grey eyes gave Smart a mere flicker of acknowledgement before she returned to waving the money at the befuddled shop assistant.

"Jeremy, did she just ignore me? Jeremy?"

Whittaker bent forwards between a melange of tatty bags for life that were hung from the wheelchair and tapped the old woman on her heavily padded coat. "I'm sorry, but we were here first."

The woman sighed. "Uh awwf," she threw over her shoulder before repeating her demand to the shop assistant whilst pointing frantically at the metal shutters that concealed the cigarettes.

As the assistant opened the shutters for the woman to demonstrate which particular brand she was after, Whittaker stood stunned. "Did she just tell me to..."

"There must be a carer somewhere." Smart was craning her neck around to see if she could spot someone. "Probably some late teenage girl mooning over the glossy mags. Let's face it, *she* can't be out on her own. The smell alone suggests she's not able to look after herself." Her nose wrinkled and she whispered, "She pongs of wee, for pity's sake. Ow!" The perfectly attired woman jumped back as the electric wheelchair lurched back and ran over her foot before scooting away and out of the superstore, almost taking a display of lemons with it as it did so.

"Finally." She marched forwards before anyone else could steal her place in the queue only to encounter a crumpled hessian bag on the floor in front of the counter.

"Looks like she dropped her shopping," the woman in the kiosk commented.

Smart gave a deep sigh and bent down to see what was lurking in the discarded carrier.

She peeled back a filthy-looking rag. "What on earth..."

Then suddenly there was a bright flash of light.

Matty Philips' ample stomach rumbled noisily from beneath his Millennium Falcon t-shirt. He just wanted to pay for the crisps he'd picked up, grab some *Rizlas* and get out. He had to meet his guy in about fifteen minutes and, at this rate, he was going to be somewhat tardy.

That was bad.

The cigarette kiosk was late opening up and there was a couple already in front of him: the bloke was some sort of hipster dude, judging by the beard that looked like it belonged on a guy from Lush, and the woman was so straight that you could use her as a guide for hanging wallpaper but she quite obviously wanted to appear hip to please the guy.

Perhaps he had a massive cock?

Philips' chuckled to himself

His mirth evaporated when an old woman zoomed her electric wheelchair into the front of the queue. She was funny looking: all grey and wrinkly under a huge over-coat and loaded down with shopping bags. Her head seemed to poke from the top of her coat without the aid of a neck.

"Weneee ee anayyy," the woman squealed at the shop assistant who had just arrived at the kiosk.

"Whoa, she's a lady Jabba!" Philips' chuckled. "Go on, say, '*Han ma bogay.*'"

She didn't. Instead, she repeated, "Weneee ee anayyy," and the woman in the kiosk looked mightily con-fused.

Philips' nerves started to get the better of him and his stomach rumbled once more. This was going to take forever! His guy was going to be so pissed off! He'd prob-ably want more for the dope. The ginger-haired stoner rummaged around in the pockets of his barely washed jeans and found all that he had in his possession: a snotty hanky, various bits of fluff, a stormtrooper mini figure and enough cash for his usual amount of weekend fun. He was going to have to improvise. Perhaps if he grabbed something from the tech department of the shop on his way out, that would pacify his dealer? He looked up and saw the crazy granny snatch up a golden box of twenty *Benson And Hedges* before shooting off quicker than Han Solo flying the Kessel Run.

"Awesome," he smiled. All he had to do now was

settle up here, grab something nice and shiny then head off.

Then suddenly there was a bright flash of light.

"Will you shut up?" Petunia Smith's son was, quite simply, doing her head in.

"I wanna *Freddo Frog*! I wanna *Freddo Frog*! I wanna *Freddo Frog*!" That's all it had been for what had seemed like the last hour but, in reality, had only been no more than sixty seconds. "I wanna *Freddo Frog*!"

Snot would be running down his face now. It always did when he started to whinge. She couldn't bear to look at him; it made her feel sick.

"I told ya, they don't have any."

He continued on with his whining litany as Petunia looked forcefully forwards at the back of some fat, ginger-haired man with body odour issues. All she wanted was to grab her fags and get out of here. She'd smoked the last one on the way down and now she was gasping for another. To take her mind off her wait, she flicked on her phone and scrolled down her messages.

"Can't wait to see you."

"I want to rip your knickers off."

"I want to eat you up."

God, that sounded good! She shivered at the thought of strong hands undressing her and a firm mouth tasting her.

"I wanna *Freddo Frog*!"

"For the last time... You've gotta be kidding!" Some old bag lady had just barged her wheelchair to the front of the queue as the kiosk had opened. "Will you stop that?" Her son was yanking frantically on her hand as his lower lip stuck out in a pout. "Quit it!" Petunia pulled back, causing the youngster to trip over his own feet and collide with the man who stood behind them; the final member of the queue. "Now see what you've done!" she yelled at her son who was now starting to build up to one of his signature siren wails. This was too much. She should have left him at home with his waste-of-space dad who sat in his underwear and scratched his balls whilst watching the footie. She wanted to get away to the sender of her text messages; she did not want to be stuck in a bloody queue waiting forever for her cigs whilst some retard got there first.

Petunia looked up at the man behind them, the one whom her brat had clouted, and started. He was dressed in an immaculate grey suit and was clean-shaven with neatly barbered hair. He would have been sexy as hell if he hadn't been looking at her son in a weird way. Reflexively she pulled her child close and his wailing stopped immediately. The man looked away from them and she followed his eyes as they tracked the bag lady hurrying out of the store, almost taking a display of lemons with her. His eyes darted to a tatty shopping bag that she had left behind and he half-smiled.

Petunia Smith felt the deepest fear that she had ever known.

Then suddenly there was a bright flash of light.

He waited at the back of the queue. There were five people in front of him: a middle-class couple of seemingly bleeding heart liberals who were actually as bigoted as Hitler's and Goebbel's love child, an overweight pot addict who was wondering if he had enough money to pay his dealer for his next fix and a self-obsessed woman who was not only cheating on her down-at-heel out-of-work husband but was also quickly regretting bringing her controlling child out when she really wanted to go and see her lover.

None of them were a threat to him.

He shifted slightly and felt the heavy weight press into his left side under his precisely cut jacket.

Soon he would have purchased his pack of *Morleys,* be back in his car and driving out of this backwater town. He knew that he was risking a lot just for a packet of cigarettes (any one of the store's video cameras could pick him up) but he had driven for ten hours overnight and he needed that rich, roasted flavour.

It was the only joy that he had left in his life these days.

The bratty child was really playing his mother up. It kept crying over and over for a *Freddo Frog* chocolate bar. Did they still make those? All his mother was concerned about were the lewd text messages that her lover had sent her that morning.

He could make life far less complicated for her. One shot and the child would be quiet. Between the eyes, close range, no chance of missing.

"Weneee ee anayyy."

The man's eyes followed the commotion at the front of the queue.

"Weneee ee anayyy."

An old, wheelchair-bound woman was harassing the young shop assistant for twenty *Benson And Hedges* but, being rather inarticulate, was struggling to get her request across. Just another day in the life of the same old, same old.

Or was it?

The wheelchair was laden down with five battered

hessian bags: four hanging to its back, the fifth in the woman's ample lap. The shop had only just opened, yet each bag seemed to be full to overflowing and dirty scraps of fabric covered whatever resided in the bottom of each bag. Clearly she had not just been shopping. Also, the bags were plastered with the logos of five different supermarkets. The one in her lap displayed the logo that adorned the wall above the kiosk that held his beloved *Morleys*, the others were branded with what the man guessed to be other local shops. As the woman leaned forward to point out her desired choice in cancer sticks, she took the bag from her lap and placed it at the foot of the counter.

The hairs on the man's neck jumped up, electrified.

Years of self-preservation screamed to him as to what was in the bag.

Then the boy of the cheating wife slapped him in the groin and his attention was distracted. It was so tempting: there was the boy, the gun was in his holster, seconds away from his hand.

Not a good idea. Not in public.

But it would sate the ravenous boredom.

As the woman followed her maternal instincts for once and pulled the boy close for futile protection, the man heard the clatter of produce as the wheelchair shopper darted out of the shop.

The bag had been left behind.

The middle-class fraud woman bent to look inside.

The man smiled as he accepted that he would not be needing his cigarettes after all.

Then suddenly there was a bright flash of light.

Maggie pulled her wheelchair to a screeching halt.

The lemons had been a close call, but she had steered around the display quite deftly. Now, outside in the car park, she fished out her phone, the one that had the over-sized buttons suitable for her trembling fingers and punched the first of five speed-dials that she had pro-grammed that morning.

It was with great satisfaction that she watched the bright flash of light and heard the cracking explosion as the glass doors of the superstore burst outwards.

Giving a small grunt of satisfaction, she pocketed the phone, pulled the second bag down into her lap and set off into town.

She had a busy morning in front of her.

Author's Notes

As I sit here, typing this on a cold February morning in 2022, I find it rather weird to think that my first book *The Casebook of Sam Spallucci* was published ten years ago. I mean, that's almost a fifth of my life spent doing something that I really enjoy — creating stories. Sure, I'd been playing around at it for many years previous. I was that kid on the playground in his own little world fighting dragons, robots and randomly made up creatures from the vivid imagination of an only child. But 2012 saw my weird ramblings finally put down in print for other people to read, and hopefully enjoy.

And enjoy them, people did!

This meant that I had people clamouring for more Sam stories. As a result, I sat down and started work on the second in the series, *Ghosts From the Past*. However, due to varied external factors, the writing of sam's second outing took longer than anticipated and, with a selection of signings appearances looming, I was stuck with rocking up with just the same book that I had taken the last time. This called for drastic action so, in the summer of 2013 I sat down and wrote my pants off. I went back to my roots as a teenager and started to pour out short stories at the rate of one a day. The result was one very tired author, but one completed short story anthology, *Oh Taste And See*. I had now doubled my portfolio!

So it continued that between each Sam Spallucci book, I would compile an anthology of short horror stories: some of them standalones, some of them expanded universe of Sam's world. A few years ago, I compiled a collection of all the Children of Cain shorts and last year I did the same with the werewolf stories that surrounded *Bloodline*, Sam's sixth adventure. I thought that, with my tenth anniversary of publication being this year, I ought to do likewise for the more horror elements of my first three anthologies. So, that is what you are currently holding in your hands.

Here are a few notes on the individual stories themselves.

Scratchcard Man:

Back in the mists of time, when I was a teenager, I devoured Steven King's *Night Shift*. I loved the short story *The Man Who Loved Flowers* which, as I recall, was the shortest tale in that book. *Scratchcard Man* is my own personal homage to that classic short story.

It is actually based on a job that I used to have when I was about fifteen. I used to go from door to door selling scratchcards, just like in the story. What I did *not* do was despatch any potential customers, honest.

Teeth:

When I wrote this short, the radio was saturated with adverts for teeth implants and I got to wondering, as one does, just how would the dentures feel about this?

Perhaps they might be a little bit miffed? Perhaps they might feel that they have been callously abandoned after years of trusty service?

Perhaps they might seek revenge?

I also find wooden marionettes somewhat creepy so the two themes just sort of fused together.

Extraction:

Not another story about dentistry, but actually a hundred-word piece I originally wrote for a competition. I never won a prize but I liked the story so decided to include it in here.

53, Bell Court:

This is my take on the bogeyman in the closet. I had a paper round when I was a kid and there was this one flat where I had to deliver papers which was exactly how I describe the one in my story. It seriously creeped me out and I always had to steel myself before going upstairs then ran like the wind without looking back afterwards. To this day it still gives me the willies!

Dog Days:

A few days before sitting down to write this one, I passed a house with a hand-written sign on its grass verge that stated in somewhat strong language what would happen if the householder caught whoever it was that was letting their dog foul there every day. As I had been asked a few weeks previous as to why I had never written a zombie story, I decided to combine the two themes.

Just beware if you kick *your* football into my yard...

Biscuit Tin Of Doom:

Here I was basically having a bit of fun and letting my mind run wild. The biscuit tin in question is actually based on one in my kitchen which I now approach with much greater caution than before.

Relic.

As with a lot of what I write, this story was based on a real event — not the escalating apocalypse, but the painting of a car in a back alley. I used to have an old, temperamental Ford Fiesta which kept getting rusty under the radiator, so one day I took a tin of gloss paint and went at it with hammer and tongs. The result was a shiny white finish on the car but various indelible splatters on the cobbles. I could have cleaned them off but I was already covered in the sticky gloop of white paint. As a result, I left the mess alone and there it remains to this day. Hopefully, no one will ever dig the cobbles up.

Test Flight.

In *Oh Taste And See* I included the hundred word piece *Extraction*. I enjoyed the challenge of creating such a short piece so much that I decided to have another go. I feel that the compact nature of the story suits quirky, little tales. I hope that you do too.

Second Time Around.

As I have mentioned before in various places, the fallen angel Asherah is one of my favourite characters. The ultimate femme fatale who can turn a collection of the dullest bank managers or accountants into the most fervent of fanatical acolytes just by the humming of a simple tune is a character who will appear time and time again in my ever-expanding universe. She is already scheduled to reappear in *Sam Spallucci: Fury of the Fallen*, a forthcoming novel regarding the fall of Troy, my magnum opus *Fallen Angel* and ultimately, after the Divergence has swept across the universe, we shall see her and her long-time companion Asmodeus riding side by side in the service of the mysterious Kanor. So I thought it only right that you had the chance to see her first appearances (*The Case Of The Fastidious Phantom* and *Sam Spallucci: Ghosts From The* Past) from her point of view.

Needs Must.

I have to say that, this is my personal favourite of my short stories to date. I wanted to create a monster with whom the reader could sympathise and come to love then pull the metaphorical rug out from under their feet right at the end. I am a great fan of the Universal *Frankenstein* movies as well as Mel Brooks' *Young Frankenstein*. In both movies, the scene with the little girl always sticks in my head. The story of Odd Bod and Emily is my little homage to that.

Just Like Everybody Else.

I have very little to say about this piece apart from the fact that you know it is true.

Prodigy.

This story was the product of two things. The first was a long coffee on a wet, windy autumn morning. I was stranded inside a coffee shop, hiding from the weather and started to doodle on a napkin. Ten minutes later I had sketched the plot for *Prodigy*. I still have the napkin somewhere. The second was a book that I was reading when I started to write *All Things Dark And Dangerous*. I am a great fan of the science fiction writer Philip K. Dick and I love the way that his approach to writing makes reality seem somewhat stilted and dull with something lurking underneath. In the book *Paycheck* there is a short story entitled *Nanny* about robot nannies that go out and battle at night. I fell in love with this tale and Dick's style so, when I started to pen *Prodigy,* I decided to follow his lead and take that dull, mundane lifestyle then flip it over to see what horror lurked underneath.

Matilda.

I am fascinated by animals and, over the years, I constantly wondered what's been going through the minds of my furry companions. As a result, I went back to this little tale that I wrote in my twenties which is about a proud feline in her last few moments and I explored what she might be feeling.

Humble Pie.

I love flash fiction. The shorter the better. I originally read this out at a Halloween event at Southcart Books in Walsall. It was enjoyed then. I hope you enjoyed it here.

Armitage.

This one, like *Prodigy*, was influenced by the style of Philip K. Dick. I constantly worry about the future of civilisation as the growing power of elite multinationals snatches power away from ineffectual governments.

My Divergent Land.

Now, if you haven't read any of my other books, you will not have had a clue as to what this little piece was about. If you have, then hopefully I have whetted your appetite for more. The Divergence is coming…

Keep safe and keep looking for what lurks in the shadows…
ASC February 2022

About The Author

A.S.Chambers resides in Lancaster, England. He lives a fairly simple life of walking in the countryside, gazing at mountains and rescuing his cat from the dastardly machinations of net curtains.

He is quite happy for, and in fact would encourage, you to follow him on Facebook, Instagram and Twitter.

There is also a nice, shiny website:
www.aschambers.co.uk